Hell is in New Jersey

by

Andy Thomas

This book was inspired by "A Souvenir of Hell," a short story by Etgar Keret.

Edited by Janice GaNun

Layout and Artwork by Ralph Eberhard

This book is dedicated to the memory of my grandfather, Richard Hannert, whose picture graces the cover of this book, to my amazing and supportive family, and to Jen, who will never let me give up on myself so matter how much I want to. Thank you for always being there for me. We will always go further.

Chapter 1

Around the turn of the twentieth century, a discovery was made that opened the doors for entrepreneurial exploitation. This is the first documentation.

June, 1909

Mr. M.H. Osborne
Woolley, PA

Dear Milton,

I find myself in improving health this morning as I write to you with a shocking development. I had every intention of writing you sooner, but, because of the wet weather, nothing could be done.

Three nights ago, I believe I discovered something that no one has ever laid eyes on. This discovery, which I admit I stumbled upon by accident, will undoubtedly make both of us rich beyond our wildest dreams.

I realize this is not the first time I have written you about a money-making endeavor, but I still feel a profit could have been turned had we just seen horse boxing to its end. It would have been as exciting a sport as has ever been imagined. I had even been working on a set of gloves for my horse, Tumble.

Let me first digress and regale you with how I came to see this miracle of nature. As you know, I have always had a taste for the drink, and, about one week ago, I found myself at a local saloon just outside of the town of Brinton, New Jersey. I was enjoying myself fine, taking full advantage of all the saloon had to offer, when it suddenly hit me that I had perhaps enjoyed myself a tad too much and needed to rid myself of the dark whiskey I had been drinking all night. Being the gentleman that I am, I decided to step out of the saloon so as not to be seen by any of the other patrons, especially those of the female persuasion, as nothing is more unattractive than a miserable drunkard who cannot hold his liquor. I went behind the bar, leaned on a tree and was set to do my evil business when I heard the chatter of other patrons coming towards me. I steadied myself and began walking into the deep woods behind the saloon, trying to get as far away as I could but close enough that I could find my way back. Unfortunately, the devil whiskey demanded that I keep walking, and, before I knew it, I was lost deep in the woods. As I tried to get my bearings, I heard a sound in the still of the shadows. It was the crackling sound of a fire burning. Thinking it may be a pack of camping vagrants, I decided to follow the sound to investigate further, but to be cautious, in case they were unfriendly or wanted by the law. Despite smelling no smoke and seeing no flames, the sound grew louder as I approached, and then I saw the sight of what I am writing to you today.

Through a break in the trees, I saw a group of people, all dressed identically in fiery, orange suits, marching in unison into a hole carved into a massive rock edifice. There must have been hundreds of them all in single file and perfectly spaced out from one another; they were marching, almost lifeless, into the bowels of the Earth. From this pitch-black hole, came the sound I heard. The crackling, searing sound of fire, breathing and pulsing, filling the otherwise still air – yet I still saw no flame.

I crept to get a closer look and then got a nostril full of the peculiar but familiar smell of burning flesh. I then deduced these people were being led by an unknown assailant into a makeshift oven and were marching towards a slow and painful death. I couldn't just sit there and watch them, so I decided to call out. "Hello," I called. "You must stop! Run away or you will surely be burned." But not a soul turned to look at me. The line of soon-to-be corpses just continued to walk towards the edifice, slowly disappearing into its mouth. I decided further action was needed, so I jumped up from my post and ran frantically towards the line of people, hoping to physically pull one away from the cavern.

Unfortunately, I had forgotten why I went out to the woods in the first place and the devil whiskey which I had gone to relieve myself of caused me to lose my balance and I tripped on a protruding tree branch and fell violently to the ground, hitting my head on a stone. Everything then went black. I awoke several hours later as the sun was just beginning to rise. My head was, of course, in a great deal of pain, but I gathered that there was no serious trauma and was able to steady myself just long enough to stand and survey my surroundings.

I looked towards the area where I saw the people walking but there was no one to be found. They had all disappeared. The massive rock face was still there, but the opening was shut tight, sealed off by some act of witchcraft. I started to think that I had just imagined the whole thing and was yet again a victim of my thirst for alcohol, but I decided to survey the area where the people walked to see if I could discover anything. I crouched down to see the unmistakable tread of a path walked over and over again – worn down shrubbery trampled on by hundreds of feet. I studied the rock face, to see if I could find the entrance in which all of the travelers disappeared, but I found no hole. When I put my hand upon the flat surface, I was startled and pulled it back immediately. The rock face was burning hot. It was then I realized I hadn't imagined a thing. What I saw was real and I knew what it was: I had discovered the underworld. I had found Hell!

Milton, I realize what I am telling you may sound like the ramblings of a drunk lunatic, but you must believe me. I know what I saw. I left the area with enough knowledge to find my way back, but kept my trail hidden enough so no one else could find it.

I need to go back, Milton, and I am asking you to go with me. I need a man like you that has a general scientific knowledge, history of traveling and, if I'm being honest, deep pockets to aid me in my quest of discovering and profiting on this phenomenon. If we play our cards right, there are ways to make a fortune with this discovery. I know you still have a lot of the money that your father left you after his passing, and I propose we use this money to further research and market what I believe to be the entrance to the underworld.

Well I guess I may as well close for this time. Please consider my request with all seriousness and send your reply as soon as you can. I want you to know that, despite my plans to turn a profit from this discovery, I am still a good Christian and, by the grace of God, I believe we will do great things.

I humbly await your reply,

G.W. Key

Almost a hundred years later, the investment flatlined.

To: bosborne@gmwdevelopments.com
From: aspears@gmdevelopments.com
Subject: Brinton Properties – Destruction
Sent: 05/11/2005

Shut it down, shut it down, shut it down! I think we both know those words are a long time coming, but we just can't sink any more money into this. This venture is bleeding us dry.
Year after year fewer and fewer people have visited "Hell's Exit," and profits have all but dried up. I think it was really the discovery of the latest Exit in Colorado that really screwed us – that's a total of 32 Exits so far, and every one is pretty much the same – a line of spacey weirdos walking aimlessly from one rock face to the other. People just don't care anymore!
The only people that seem to give a shit are the throngs of religious nuts who set up makeshift shrines and get into fights with each other all of the time - I am so sick of breaking up fights between the churchies and the Devil worshippers. It's private property for fucks sake. They're lucky I don't shoot them.
We should have taken everyone's advice and tried to designate it as a historic landmark while we had the chance. Do you still have that contact for the NPS I sent you a while ago?
We need to pull our money out of any business or attraction associated with Hell's Exit in Brinton or anywhere else we may have foolishly invested. You need to sell the land and every failing business on it, including that stupid gift shop. I understand that the Outer Shell gift shop was opened by your great-grandfather and it means a lot to you, but I don't think it's worth the eventual financial hemorrhaging that it will surely cause. I strongly urge you to do the reasonable thing

and close up shop immediately, regardless of emotional attachment.

We all thought this would one day make us money. We thought it was a phenomenon, and maybe in some small way it is, but I think we need to stop kidding ourselves and turn it over to the people who know what to do with it. I'm sure we'll have several more conversations about the logistics of dismantling these ventures, but, for now, please make the preliminary arrangements and I will be in touch.

Talk soon,

Alan

To: aspears@gmdevelopments.com
From: bosborne@gmwdevelopments.com
Subject: Re: Brinton Properties – Destruction
Sent: 5/12/05

Alan, I will start contacting the necessary parties about our financial bailouts from the discussed businesses, but I will not sell the land or the gift shop for that matter. It all means too much to me. The Hell's Exits are mine and always will be. They can have the land over my dead body.

I will be in touch regarding other matters.

Ben

Chapter 2

One year after the financial dismantling, only the gift shop remains. This is the story of the only remaining employee and his eventual descent into the underworld.

It wasn't the amount of blood that concerned Dylan James; it was the color of it. When the nosebleeds started, the blood was a bright, crimson fluid, alive and spirited like the sunrise. Now it poured out of his nostril and hit the shower floor in a dull, burnt orange, depressed and breathless, like his body was slowly dying. Depending on who he talked to, the nosebleeds persisted due to a myriad of issues: stress, poor diet, too much alcohol, lack of faith in God. Dylan didn't know why this particular bout had started, but he needed it to stop soon or he would be late for work.

Outside of his cramped apartment was a hazy day in the town he had spent his entire life in, Brinton, NJ. He knew from time to time the sun came out, but he couldn't remember when the last time was. So, with no urgency to immerse himself into another one of Brinton's depressing days, he decided to sit down, lower his head and let the blood pool into small red discs on the shower floor. He had started working at the Outer Shell gift shop when he turned 18. At the time, it was a stop-gap job and would give him a little bit of money before he decided what college he would go to, but he never did make that decision. Now at age 29, he felt he was already out of options. So four or five days a week, depending on how hung over he was, he went through the same daily routine of sitting in the shower and wondering what stupid questions he was going to be asked today: How many people come out of the Exit daily? Where are they going? Where's the Devil? Is there a God?

Why am I such an asshole? (OK, maybe no one ever asked Dylan this, but he really wished they did.) While Dylan knew the answer to some of these questions, he just could not stand answering them over and over and over again.

Then there were the religious freaks who infested the area who rarely asked questions but just sat around and waited for answers. For years they had been waiting, but the answers never came. People kept waiting for a deeper meaning, but all they got was a line of unblinking, silent, dead people.

As far as anyone knew, no one had ever gotten into Hell, and nothing new could be learned, yet still some people kept coming. Unfortunately, few of them ever bought anything.

The pipes in Dylan's building were old and unpredictable, and he could feel the water getting colder. He ran his index finger under his nose to check for blood and saw that there was none. The cooling water knocked some life back into him, reminding him that, although he hated his job, it was all he had and could not afford to get fired. He stood up, turned the knob hard to the right and got out of the shower. He wiped steam off of the mirror and looked hard at his reflection. A trickle of blood shot from his nostril. He wasn't going anywhere.

He was ten minutes late opening up Outer Shell, but he was confident no one noticed. The owner, Ben Osborne, who had inherited the business from his father, John, whose father, Milton had first discovered the entrance to Hell, popped in occasionally to take the small amount of money made each week to the bank, but it was not uncommon for Dylan to go several weeks without seeing him. This, Dylan believed, was one of the few perks of his job. Dylan took the heavy padlock off the store's steel shutters and lifted them to reveal a glass storefront with the business name etched in black stencil over the windows and doors. He unlocked and opened the front door and heard the familiar chime of the bell hitting the door frame to alert him that customers were entering the store. He hated that sound.

He put on a pot of coffee, counted the meager amount of money in the safe and took his place on a stool behind the counter. After fifteen minutes and not a single customer, he decided this long day would become significantly shorter if he was drunk; he needed beer.

He repeated the process he had just gone through, only in reverse, locking the door behind him and closing the metal shutter over the window. Although he knew he was only going to be gone a few minutes, the steel shutters had become pretty imperative as, due to a further decrease in property value in the area, it was not uncommon for buildings in the area to be broken into. Most of the businesses in the area had closed long ago, and the area was full of boarded up storefronts, abandoned houses and vacant buildings. Dylan had learned to move swiftly and cautiously by these skeletal structures, as packs of stray dogs had taken to moving in and attacking unsuspecting people passing by.

Dylan believed it was one more delicious layer of shit piled on to the proverbial shit cake that was the town of Brinton. "What's that? You don't think your life in this town can get any worse? Hey, watch out for that pack of hungry, ferocious dogs!" The town had undergone a dramatic facelift since its early boom when the Hell Exits were discovered and the whole state was abuzz with its unlimited potential. By the time Dylan was born however, all that potential had been sucked away, and Brinton had been in a constant state of economic turmoil, leaving those who grew up there with very little sense of purpose or drive.

He ran quickly by a vacant building on Orchard, shook off a homeless man on Wilchard, tripped on a pothole crossing Downing and entered his favorite liquor store on the corner of 10th and Ashland. There were several liquor stores in the area, but Dylan preferred this particular one because of the entertainment that its usual clerk supplied. Easy Money was not his Christian name, but that is what everyone called him. Dylan was not sure why. A one-of-a-kind spirit if there ever was one, Easy Money was a black man in his late thirties with a fiery red afro. Dylan had heard him tell customers before that he was African Irish, and if they didn't like it, they could fuck off. Easy Money did not suffer fools and was in constant screaming matches with his customers. He yelled at pretty much every one except Dylan.

As Dylan entered the store, he saw Easy Money in his usual place behind the counter and its bulletproof glass. He was already engaged in an argument. "Nah, hell no," he bellowed to a pair of twenty something Hispanic men. "No cash back, no cash back at all youngin's! Keep that shit up and you'll catch me on the 6:00 news," Easy Money mimed that he was shooting a gun in the air. Dylan wasn't exactly sure what Easy Money meant, but it seemed to be effective as the two men gave up and turned towards the exit. "Yeah, that's right. Y'all can't see me. I'm from East St. Louis, I don't play around."

Dylan was next, so he approached the counter. As per usual when he saw Dylan, he immediately changed his tone. "Ah shit, what's up, baby?" It had been like this ever since Dylan could remember. Easy Money took offense to every customer he had, except Dylan. "Not much man, how you doing?" Dylan responded.
"Oh you know me, baby. I'm always good, as long as the sun be shining I'll be alright. One day you'll realize that too Dylan, and stop walking around moping and shit all the time! That'll be $16.50, my man." Easy Money was always giving Dylan pearls of wisdom like this. Although he felt he did have a bleak world view, he didn't think he carried himself as such. Easy Money, however, always knew when something was wrong.
"You always know how to make me feel better, Easy," Dylan said

handing him a twenty. "It's like you're my guardian angel or something."

Easy Money palmed Dylan's money and stared at him hard. "What kinda dumb shit is that?" He said. "Fucking guardian angel? Motha fucka don't bring that shit up in my store. You better get your head right Dylan."

"Yeah, you're right man. Just thinking out loud. Thanks again." Dylan snatched his change from Easy Money's hands and headed back out of the store. From inside he heard him shouting again "Who the fuck is next?!"

Dylan wandered back to the gift shop. He was sipping beer that he had poured into a 7-11 Big Gulp cup and watching the Line of people coming out of Hell from the outdoor porch on the side of the Outer Shell gift shop. Although most people had lost interest in "the travelers," he found himself still strangely fascinated by them. He made up back stories for most of them, even inventing dialects and mannerisms for them. He had watched the Line so frequently that he often saw the same travelers come back through the Line and had developed a certain affinity for some of them, one in particular.

He was in the middle of scanning the Line when he heard that familiar ding of the front door being opened. He sighed, set down his beer and walked inside to his post behind the counter. Inside he was greeted by a portly man in a collared shirt, cargo shorts and crocs. The man looked befuddled.

"Morning," Dylan half-heartedly greeted him.

"Is it?" the man responded. "It's so dark here."

"So I've heard. I think it's so their eyes can adjust."

"They?" the man asked.

"Yeah. You know, them," Dylan said as he motioned to the Line of travelers. "It's gotta be dark down there in...HELL," Dylan said in his best Ernest Borgnine voice.

"Oh yeah," said the man as he walked towards the window to get a closer look at the slow, sad march. "Where are they going?"

"I don't know," Dylan said, fielding the question for possibly the ten thousandth time. "Maybe to a Mets game."

"I heard that Hell is so full that the Devil is releasing people back into the world so he can let new ones in," the man said, still looking out the window. "That's why the crime rate has gone back up. All those evil people are returning to the world and committing the same sins that got them there in the first place. It's really sick."

"Could be," said Dylan. "Why don't you go ask 'em?"

"Oh, I wouldn't dare consort with people like that," the man said turning to face Dylan. "Best leave some things be, eh?"

"Eh," Dylan responded in affirmation.

The man then turned from the counter and started perusing the merchandise. Dylan watched him laboriously survey price tag after price tag. He regretted not bringing his beer inside. Finally the man stood on his tippy toes and awkwardly plucked a shirt off a rack before displaying it to Dylan.

"Do you have this in an XXL?" the customer asked holding up a black t-shirt that read, "BRINTON: It's Not Hell, But It's Close."

Four hours later, Dylan was on his fourth beer, which made him content but was not making the time go by any quicker. He was thinking he could close up early when he heard the ding from the front door again. He looked through the window and saw that it was John Tate, his longtime friend who came into the store almost every day and had never purchased anything. The two had grown up together, becoming lifelong friends after Dylan had punched him in the face during a third grade shoving match. Dylan had cut his hand open on John's tooth and had to get stitches so the two reconciled that they were even. They bonded that summer over their mutual love of BB guns and zombie movies. Their relationship hadn't changed much over the years, as they still got together and watched bad horror movies on a weekly basis, only now they did it with booze. Dylan still punched John in the face from time to time.

Dylan caught John's attention through the window and motioned for him to come outside and join him on the porch. John dodged a few display racks, slid the sliding glass door open and stepped into the dismal Brinton morning.

"Hey man," John said lazily.

"Hey," Dylan replied. "What's going on?"

"Oh, you know, same old. Hurting pretty bad." John responded extending a shaky hand to Dylan.

Dylan recoiled in mock horror.

"Jesus, dude, you smell like a brewery."

"Oh, yeah, sorry, Jenelle and I went out last night. Things got a little hazy towards the end."

"That's still happening, huh?" Dylan asked with a smirk on his face.

"I really like her man," John responded sheepishly. "I mean, we get along great, she's funny, we have a great time together. It's just that sexually she's just…bleh. I can't do it unless I'm blackout drunk. I think we did stuff last night, but I can't remember."

"Look man, if you're not attracted to her, you need to let her know," Dylan admonished. "What you're doing is not healthy, physically or mentally."

"Yeah, I know," John said scratching his head. "I'll figure it out one of these days, but as long as there's whiskey in the world, Jenelle and I will be just fine."

"That's just sad," Dylan replied.

"Not as sad as working at a gift shop for 11 years." It was silent for several seconds before John finally said, "Sorry dude, that was a low blow."

"It's OK. I get it. Sometimes I think I'd be better off marching off into nothing like these assholes," Dylan said motioning at the current wave of "travelers."

John took a long look at the weary Line, surveying them intently for a few moments. "You see her yet?" he asked.

"Not yet," Dylan said. "She should be through today though. It's been a week since I last saw her, and she usually comes through on Monday...." Dylan trailed off, knowing that he was saying too much. "But, I'm not totally sure who you're referring to."

"Ha! Come on, man. Who do you think you're talking to? The dead chick. The one you are always staring at."

"Oh her. No, not yet."

"Don't you think being in love with a girl you've never talked to is a little strange? Like way stranger than my situation? I mean, my infatuation is based purely on booze, sure, but, yours is based on…well, nothing."

Dylan shot John a sharp look.

John threw up his hands in mock surrender.

"I'm not in love with her, I'm just intrigued," Dylan paused trying to muster up some sense of rationale. "There's something about her that I like. She seems...different."

"I get it man. She's a hot, dead chick. What's not to like? But don't you think this has more to do to do with Monica pissing all over your heart? Maybe you're a little vulnerable right now?"

"I don't want to talk about that," Dylan shot back.

The two sat in awkward silence for a few moments until Dylan reached under his chair and pulled out a conciliatory beer, handing it to John.

"Hell yeah," John said before cracking it open and taking a long pull.

The two took turns taking sips while the Line of orange-suited travelers walked together, resembling the flat, blurred line of a heart monitor.

"You gonna try to talk to her again?"

"Who? Monica? Fuck no. I'm done with that girl."

"No, not Monica! Deady McHotty Pants. "

"Oh her," Dylan said sitting back in his chair. "Yeah, I think I'm gonna try."

Chapter 3

The line outside of counselor Jay Stevenson's office was almost as long as the one protruding from the mouth of Hell. Stevenson had served as Hell counselor for the better part of 45 years and had just recently really started to excel at his job. It was his responsibility to talk to people about the daily stresses of living in the underworld.

On the surface, people usually went to therapy for superficial reasons. An unloving father or the aftermath of a divorce were nothing when compared to the torturous rigors hand-picked for each person that was unlucky enough to be sent through Hell's portal. A common misconception about Hell is that it is all fire and brimstone, whips and chains, torture and pain, but this is not accurate.

The complexion of Hell is composed of individual annoyances that nicked away at the very core of each person when they were alive. Did you have road rage before you arrived? Then for five hours in Hell you would be forced to sit in traffic, inching towards a destination that you would never reach and would always be late for. Sometimes, people would have to sit in traffic while all the other cars were empty. Highways extended through different sections of Hell, but for some reason, no matter how far you drove, you would end up right back where you started. The Hell of trying to find something you lost was a popular torture as hundreds of Inhabitants would be made to think they needed to find that extra sock or their keys and would frantically dash from room to room as their mind slowly slipped away. Other tortures, such as not being able to open the window to the width you want it to without it slipping back down and watching people push the hair on their eyebrows against the grain were not as common, but were equally as effective.

The counselor's office was as drab and typical as you would expect. This too was by design, and most of Hell looked very similar. Rows and rows of partitions protruded out of otherwise rocky walls and stretched endlessly, being broken up only by malfunctioning printers, fax machines and coffee makers as the persistent whir of each machine echoed off the hollow walls. It was Jay Stevenson's job to talk to the Inhabitants about how these tortures made them feel but never his job to rectify it – it was difficult.

Although Stevenson had his regular clients, many of Hell's Inhabitants chose to deny his help and, just like people on the surface, suppress their problems to the point of complete and utter disillusionment, causing them to "kill" themselves. In Hell this only caused you to immediately reappear through the Admissions Portal - only shorter. Each botched attempt, knocked four inches off the Inhabitant's height. Daniel Sherman, a ball of fury and emotion both in death and life, had yet to figure this out and, after three suicide attempts, now stood a paltry three feet two inches tall, relegating him as one of the Inhabitants' few sources of comedy in their otherwise dismal world.

Despite most Inhabitant's refusal to take counselor Jay's therapeutic advice, his office was always full of visitors. This was due in large part to the fact that he was in charge of handing out surface passes. Surface passes allowed Inhabitants to go out to the surface, i.e., Earth, for an allotted time. Not unlike prison, it was based on good behavior, severity of crimes they had committed while living and overall general disposition. The only other way to leave the underworld was to exchange five surface passes for a "haunting." This was pretty much what you'd imagine it was. It allowed the spirit of the Inhabitant, but not the remade body, to return to the surface to "visit" someone from their life on Earth. Many people used it to say goodbye to a loved one or deliver a message from beyond the grave. But most people just used it to scare the shit out of people they didn't like when they were alive. This was Hell after all, and the majority of people down there were dicks.

Despite the criteria, Jay was liberal with surface passes. Unlike a lot of people in the underworld, he had had a pure soul and was truly empathetic. On Earth he was a high school guidance counselor, offering oft-ignored career advice to unenthusiastic freshman and sophomores. He was fair and patient with them, and really did care about their future. Kids, however, are cruel, and Jay constantly found himself the butt of juvenile jokes, usually involving leftover cafeteria food and the tailpipe of his car. One Sunday afternoon, Jay attended his book club meeting at his friend Barbara's house. The wine served at the party was delicious and seemingly bottomless. Jay, who did not consider himself a big drinker, before too long was very, very drunk. Not wanting to embarrass himself, he decided to make an early exit and drive home. While he was driving past the school, he swerved to avoid a darting dog, lost control and plowed into the side of the school. He died instantly. He took three promising freshman girls with him, who had just gotten home from a late night volleyball game and were waiting for their parents to pick them up. When he awoke, he was in Hell.

Another of Hell's many Inhabitants, Lauren Adams, was waiting to talk to Jay hoping to receive one of the coveted surface passes. In Hell, there is a lot of waiting. You wait to be tortured, you wait to be screamed at and sometimes you wait just to wait, all the while still feeling that anxious annoyance that people feel when waiting in line at the DMV. Waiting is a miserable experience on Earth and sometimes, in Hell, people wait for things for hundreds of years. What it really boils down to is that Hell is extremely tedious. Lauren couldn't tell how long she had been waiting to see the counselor, because, as you can guess, people start to lose their ability to conceptualize time in Hell, besides the fact that there are few clocks.

"Been waiting long?" Lauren heard a voice ask behind her. Lauren turned to see the source of the voice and was saddened to see it was Artie Ferner, standing there trying to look flirtatious and, as per usual, sweating profusely and bleeding slightly from his head.

"What happened to your head?" she responded without bothering to exchange pleasantries.

"God damn it!" Artie barked, reaching into his back pocket to retrieve a red bandana that he used to dap gingerly at the open wound. "It's that fucking window again. They say once I get it to open at exactly four and three-quarter inches, then I can go home, back to Scotch Plains. Every time I come close, something shifts and it either slams shut or comes shooting upwards. I almost had it today."

"You do realize you will never get it open to four and three-quarter inches, right Artie? The harder you try, the more they sit back and laugh at you. That's your torture Artie."

"They told me that my torture hadn't come in yet and that this was just a task to prove my worth."

"How long have you been here Artie?" Lauren asked.

"About fifteen years."

"Maybe in another fifteen you'll figure out how things work down here."

Artie had been a thorn in Lauren's side ever since she arrived in Hell six years ago. A constant source of annoyance, Artie had made it his personal mission to try and sleep with Lauren. Sex was one of the few pleasures Hell allowed. With his constant sweating, comb over and general pungent smell, Lauren knew it would be a cold day in Hell before she even considered sleeping with Artie and it hadn't dipped below 120 since her arrival. There were a lot of bad people in Hell, but Lauren considered Artie the absolute worst.

On Earth, Artie had been a scum bag as well. He had a hard time hearing the word no. One night, he decided to sneak into the house of a woman he had been eyeballing almost every day at the grocery store where he worked. As he crept in the window, he slipped and crashed into a recycling bin filled with beer bottles. The girl's boyfriend, startled and drunk, beat Artie to death with the tail end of the 32 ounce bottle of High Life he was finishing up. Artie woke up in Hell. The boyfriend claimed self-defense, never served time and later received oral sex from the girl.

"So anyway, how long you been waiting?"

"Couple of hours I guess," Lauren guessed.

"Couple of hours, huh," Artie began. "Boy, I tell you, I can think of something else we could have been doing for all that time. And believe me, it would've lasted the whole time."

Lauren kept her back to Artie, hoping he would just tire himself out on his own.

"Ya hear that? The whoooole time, Lauren. Pleasure for every second of every..."

"I heard you Artie!" Lauren exploded, cutting off Artie and any further disgusting thing he could say. "This is neeeeeeeever gonna happen! I don't care if we're both here for 500 years. I will never, ever, ever sleep with you. Got it?!" Lauren wasn't always this quick to yell at people. But Hell has a way of changing people and she could feel herself growing angrier by the day.

"Geeze baby, doll," Artie said trying to calm Lauren down. "I get it. You're annoyed and cranky. I'm just trying to bring a little sunshine into your life. What's the matter, afraid you'll fall in love?"

Lauren turned slowly and methodically towards Artie. "I've been in love before," she explained very slowly to Artie. "And this is where it got me. So, to answer your question; yes, I am afraid to fall in love, but not with you, You sicken me."

"Sometimes people need to get a little sick in the sack," Artie said.

"I have no idea what that means," Lauren said turning away again, "but if you keep bothering me I will rip your sick little sack clean off."

   The line shifted forward and Lauren was pleased with herself as she seemed to shut Artie up for the time being. "Fucking men," she thought. They were nothing but trouble.

Unbeknownst to her, on the surface, a man she had never met before, was waiting for her arrival.

Chapter 4

"Some lady tried to kick my ass again last night," John said to Dylan after a few moments of silence. The two were sitting on the porch of the Outer Shell, watching the Line. Each had finished about six beers, which was a usual occurrence for the two. One time he and John had gotten so drunk on whiskey that Dylan didn't remember closing the store, and, when he got there the next day, all the money from the register was in the bathroom sink and he had written "Sundance Kid" in sharpie on the mirror. To this day he still had no recollection of doing it but figured it had something to do with a conversation the two had gotten into about how robbing a stagecoach wouldn't be that hard. After that, Dylan had to invoke the "no whiskey until after 5:00 rule."

"Again, because of the blog?"
"Because of the blog," John explained. The blog that John and Dylan were referring to was something that John had started months earlier called "The Art of Sneaking." After watching *The Departed*, while drunk, John and Dylan concluded that Leonardo DiCaprio could have easily caught Matt Damon if his sneaking skills were a little better. "Jesus dude, he's banging into trash cans and shit!" John exclaimed at the time. That night the two concluded that they were so stealthy and cat-like that they could follow anyone without the suspect noticing their presence at all.
A half bottle of Jack Daniels later and John and Dylan found themselves following a night dishwasher at IHOP back to his apartment. After about a mile, most likely due to John burping every few steps, the dishwasher noticed he was being followed, sprayed off a shot of pepper spray into the air and ran off into the

night screaming "Help!" John and Dylan turned and ran the other way before Dylan lost his balance and ran head first into a trash can – oh, the irony.

The next day, after he had sobered, Dylan vowed to never follow anyone again. John, on the other hand, decided to make this a weekly occurrence and blog about his experiences. "The Art of Sneaking," as he decided to name it, had gotten John punched in the stomach by a 12-year-old, called a pervert by a barista and, on one occasion, run over by a Vespa scooter.

Dylan was glad to see his friend's enthusiasm for the blog hadn't waned.

"I'm telling you, man, humans are not far off from animals when it comes to protecting their kids," John said. "This woman last night came after me like a God damned lioness protecting her cubs, took off her shoe and everything. I almost took a stiletto right in the eye."

"I'm glad you're still doing this man," Dylan mocked. "It sounds very rewarding."

"Just wait, dude, people love reading idiotic shit on the Internet," John said. "You ever see that website *A Life of Head Ons?*' This dude purposely gets in car wrecks and then writes about them later. He got his own TV show. At least he had one. I think it got canceled, actually. Somebody sued. Regardless, that, my friend, is where I'm headed, and you can either come along for the ride or sit around here drinking beers!"

"Want another one?" Dylan asked.

"That's a stupid question," John said happily accepting his friends offer, "You just wait Dylan. I'm gonna make enough money to leave this shithole town far behind, and, if the little doggie here is nice, I may even toss behind a couple scraps."

"Oh please don't forget the little people."

"Wouldn't dream of it."

The two shared a laugh, clinked their cans together and took a collective swig. As per usual, after moments like this, an awkward silence followed as the two looked off into nothing. The Line of people had dissipated, experiencing a lull as it did from time to time.

"How's your mom doing? Is she still, ya know, not all there," John asked while making the universal symbol of crazy, slowly circling his index finger around his ear.

"She's not crazy, man, she's sick. She has a disease. I've told you this before."

"Yeah I know, she has Werthers-something. I thought you said it makes her crazy?"

"I never said that…maybe I did…I don't know. It's not Werthers, she's not a butterscotch. I think she's still all there, she just can't tell anyone if she is. To answer your question, I think she's getting worse."

The affliction that Dylan's mom was suffering from was Expressive Wernicke's Aphasia, a neurological disorder that caused her to mix up her speech, sometimes reciting entire sentences without a single actual word.

Everything had changed for Dylan and his family when he was twelve and a semi-truck ran a red light and plowed into the car that was carrying Dylan and his parents. His father died instantly, his mother was left with severe head trauma and Dylan miraculously escaped completely unscathed. It took the doctor's a few months to accurately diagnose what was wrong with Dylan's mom, Grace. Dylan always thought the term was a euphemism for what it really was: brain damage. In the aftermath of his father's death, Dylan was left with a mother that, while clearly crippled by sadness, had very little means to communicate her sorrow to people. This led to many letters left on the kitchen table for Dylan to read. This was her only real way to communicate, but, due to the disease, the letters were difficult to decipher as well. Grace had been on disability since the accident and lived alone.

Dylan had known John before the accident and John never gave up on him. There were times when Dylan wondered if he really liked his old friend, but he knew that whether he did or not, there was no getting rid of him.

"When are you gonna go see her again?" John asked

"I think tomorrow after work. She has another appointment with her pathologist, and I told her I'd pick her up. I gotta stop and get groceries for her on the way over. You want to roll with me to the store? I can drop you off after, on the way to the hospital."

"Yeah, sounds good," John said. "I have to pick up some stuff anyway. Shit, remember that time I shot a bb gun at the front of your house and shattered that huge bay window? Your mom flew out of the house and came at me with a dust buster. Ha! I'll never forget that scream – Joooooooohhhhhny!"

"I don't remember that," Dylan said.

"Really, how can you forget that? We were like 10 years old, she made you pay for half of it!"

Dylan shrugged, took a nervous sip of beer and said, "I don't remember anything about my mom before the accident. To me, she's always been this way."

John, realizing the weight of the situation, looked at Dylan and offered the only words of condolences he could think of. "Oh man. That sucks."

"How much longer are we open for?" John asked. "Let's get the fuck out of here and go get some wings and more beer."

"I like how you say 'we' like you work here," Dylan responded.

"Just because you're here every day doesn't mean you get paid. By

my count you've cost this store far more money than you've made
for it, considering all the crap you've broken."

"Well, maybe you shouldn't put the snow globes next to the
bathroom. That's an accident just waiting to happen."

"While that may be true, 'we' gotta keep the store open for a
couple more hours, some very important customer may need to
purchase one of the aforementioned snow globes. Also, I'm
curious to see who else shows up in the line."

"Ah ha!" John blurted out. "So you are waiting for her! I knew it."

"Yeah, you got me Sherlock, congrats."

"Do you even know her name?"

"No," Dylan began. "I haven't mustered up the courage to really
say anything to her yet. I think today might be the day though."

"You get weirder and weirder every day," John said.

Dylan paused for a second and opened his mouth to dispute John's
point, before realizing his friend was right. He sat back in his chair
and took a big sip of beer.

"Hey look, it's starting again." John pointed off in the distance as
the rock wall, Hell's Exit, was slowly opening. A few random
tourists got out their cameras and started snapping pictures as a
few travelers emerged from the hole looking bedraggled, beaten
down and totally and utterly uninteresting.

"Yep, that's it, people," John said. "That's literally all you're
gonna see. They just keep walking. Shoulda went to Disneyland.
Hey, look who it is."

"What? Do you see her?" Dylan asked.

"Nope, sorry man. Just that guy we see all of the time, The Kid."

John and Dylan had watched the line so much while drinking, that
it was not uncommon for them to see people more than once.
When they became familiar with certain travelers, they started
giving them nicknames. There was Gumby, a man they noticed

after John observed that he walked "rubbery." Stumpy Pete was a man that couldn't have been more than three feet tall, and then there was this man, The Kid, called so because he looked shockingly similar to Kid from the 80s rap duo Kid & Play, the same high faded flat top and everything.

"I wonder what he did that landed him down there? He seems so cool."

"Seems cool?" Dylan began. "Why does he seem cool? Is it because he's black and you have this strange obsession with black people?"

"I just want them to like me," John said.

"That's racist, man," Dylan said.

"How is it racist if you want people to like you?"

"Because, John, you aren't appreciating people for their individuality. You think that if you get one black friend, then the whole race of black people will be magically obligated to like you, and you can walk around and show them off to people like a God damned side show. This is why any black person I know and consider a friend I keep far away from you, because you creep them out with your skewed view on race."

Dylan turned to John to see if any of this was sinking in.

He was asleep.

Chapter 5

Lauren had finally arrived at counselor Stevenson's office and was seated at his desk waiting for him to finish a phone call. The track lighting, which was everywhere in Hell, blinked sickly above her. In front of her, seated behind a large, cluttered, wooden desk, the counselor was talking on the phone.

"What's the severity of the damage?" he asked someone on the other line. "And you think he did it intentionally....yeah." He held up a finger in Lauren's direction letting her know it'd only be another minute. He was a short man with thick black glasses, perched atop a thick nose which was slightly obscured by a bushy mustache. "Well, I hope it grows back. Let me know how I can help. Buh-bye now."

The counselor hung up the phone and again held his finger up to Lauren as he wrote something with his free hand into a planner. "Just a second," he said to himself without looking up "...aaaand, we're clear. What can I do for you? Wait, don't tell me, a surface pass, right?

"Ummm, yeah," Lauren began,. "Yeah, I'd love one."

"OK then," the counselor began. "I think we can do that for you. Do you have your written request?"

Lauren reached into the front pocket on her jumpsuit and retrieved a crumpled yellow piece of paper which she handed to the counselor.

"Okay, great," The counselor said while surveying the form making sure everything was filled out properly. "It looks like everything is in order. And you have been to the surface before, so you're familiar with the rules, right? No stepping out of Line, no talking to anyone, only looking up every 200 steps, yada, yada, yada."

Lauren responded with an affirming nod. Lauren was very familiar with these rules, as she had tried to break the first one before. On her first visit to the outside world, Lauren had immediately made a break for it and started running into the nearby woods by Brinton. She thought she had made a clean getaway, and, having nowhere to go, she decided to lay down by a lightning-struck tree. She fell asleep and when she woke up she was back in Hell. She had no recollection of how she got there and couldn't explain how she got back. What she learned from this experience was that there was no escape. Later that day, a group of Hell's guards found her asleep in her bunk, dragged her from the room and tortured her by making her read all of Ayn Rand's *Atlas Shrugged,* her least favorite book of all time, six times in a row, out loud. Worse, was that they warned her that a second escape attempt would result in the surface pass privilege being revoked entirely. This was not a risk that anyone, including Lauren, was willing to take.

"Whoopsy, it looks like you left one part blank," The counselor said, turning the form to face Lauren. "You didn't write anything here when it asks the reason for being condemned in the first place. What was the nature of your offense that brought you here?" Lauren shifted uncomfortably in her seat.

"Suicide, I guess, and, um...murder."

Jay, unfazed by Lauren's admission, finished filling out the necessary paperwork and excused himself for a staff meeting. Once a week he was forced to sit through these wretched staff meetings and go over rules and regulations, torture tactics and, of course, the number of surface passes given in a quarter. Every meeting he was told to give out fewer passes, but he just didn't have it in his heart to deny someone a chance to return to the outside world, even if for a few moments.

He gazed listlessly at the front of the room while a massive lump of a guard everyone called Brick went over security and restraint tactics for the third time this month.

"So, in summation," he droned on, "if the Inhabitant is resisting and further force is needed, simply grab a hold of their upper extremities and twist back like so." Jay watched as an Inhabitant, forced into volunteering, had his arms bent backward in an extremely forceful manner by Brick until a loud pop was heard and the volunteer suddenly passed out and went limp in the Brick's arms. He then dropped him to the floor and, looking pleased with himself, proudly looked at the staff before him. "As you see, the Inhabitant is now completely... incapa...indecapite-ted...passed out, and can now be taken safely to his initial point of destination."

The staff, knowing that the presentation was over, gave out a scattered round of applause, while two more guards picked the volunteer off the floor and dragged him out of the room.

"OK, great, just great," said Neville Black, rising to his feet and still clapping slowly. "Does anyone have any questions for Brick?" he asked while looking around the room. "If you do, please remember to speak slowly so he can follow along." No one raised their hands. "Okay, well let's give him one more round of applause."

Neville Black, although slim and frail in appearance, was one of the highest ranking officials in Hell. He was the Devil's right hand man, his personal assistant or, as most people called him, his little bitch. Neville, unaware of people's opinion of him, often thought of himself as equally as important and feared as the Devil. This was slightly true, because in actuality not many people respected the Devil either.

Neville wore the same tweed suit every day, and no one knew exactly how he ended up in Hell.

"That will conclude the regulations part of our meeting. I think we're all up to speed on that, right? Good," Neville said before pausing for a long drink of water. "As promised," he continued, "we have a special treat for you today. The Devil himself has found time to come down here and speak with you today. Those of you in this room should consider yourself very privileged. So, without further ado, I introduce to you the Lord of the Underworld and my best friend, Satan!"

Just then, the track lighting in the conference room darkened and plumes of black smoke were released from the walls.

"Here we go again," Jay thought to himself.

A slow rumble shook the walls, while red spirals of fire shot violently up from the floor. Up at the front of the room, Neville Black began stomping out the cadence to Queen's "We Will Rock You" while prompting the rest of the staff to do the same. The staff lethargically stomped along while Neville gently strummed an air guitar to a piped-in track playing a solo of truly epic proportions. An explosion of sparks and smoke left the whole room dark for a moment, and, when it cleared, there was the Devil.

He marched into the room slowly and clumsily, his arm was clasping a red cape that he held up over his mouth in a feeble attempt to mask his identity. After he walked in place for a few moments, his arms shot out in a Christ-like pose, spreading his cape apart like two giant wings. He spun around a few times, revealing that "Hail Satan" was written in black on the inside of the cape and a giant pentagram decorated the back of it.

Neville Black now prompted the room to clap louder and stand to give the Devil an ovation. They reluctantly agreed.

"Silence!" the Devil shouted to the barely audible audience, prompting Mr. Black to stop the audio on the guitar track and bow his head. "I have arrived! You may be seated."

Jay Stevenson sat down and hoped the theatrics were over.

The Devil sure knew how to make an entrance.

Chapter 6

Dylan heard the ding of the front door and went inside to see who it was. "Fifth customer of the day," he thought, "must be some kind of record." He looked at his watch and saw that the store was supposed to close in 15 minutes and wondered what law of physics made it possible for customers to come in just when businesses were trying to close. If it was Murphy, he was going to find him and kill him. He looked over at John who was still fast asleep clutching a half-full beer.

Dylan sighed heavily and went inside.

Once inside he saw that it wasn't a customer at all, but Jim Collins, a friend of his from high school whom he still played fantasy football with. He was holding a cup of coffee and a newspaper.

"Hey, what's up man?" Dylan greeted him. "Sorry if I kept you waiting, I thought you were a customer."

"Ha! Nice. Good to hear you're still in the running for employee of the year."

"I'm the only employee they have. That'll have to suffice for now - what's up?"

"Oh nothing, I was just...have you been drinking?"

"Only a couple...maybe a little...ya need something?"

"Ha! No judgment here man. I just popped in to ask you if you heard the latest on David?" The David that Jim was referring to was their mutual childhood friend David Estern. The three of them, along with John, were best friends growing up. Like friends tend to do sometime, they all drifted their own ways, and Dylan had eventually lost touch with him. He had all but forgotten about him when a few years back Dylan saw David's name in the front page of the local paper. He had brought a gun into Summerside Mall and killed twelve people including a five year old girl.

"Well, no, I guess nothing recently. What's the word?"

"They're killing him," Jim said.

"Well, yeah, I knew that already. The trial's been over for awhile now. Lethal injection. That's rough."

"No I mean it's actually happening. They're executing him on Saturday."

"Wow," Dylan said, averting his eyes from Jim's and staring at the counter. "I can't believe it's actually happening. I mean there's nothing else to be done?"

"Well, he's waived all of his appeals, has done so for the last couple years. It seems like he's ready for it. I read in the paper that there's a prison shrink still causing a stink, but there's a slim chance he'll be able to do anything."

"I still wonder about what he was thinking, ya know. He was always such a happy kid. Whatever made him do that is just so crazy."

"You know it is, right?" Jim said.

"What do you mean?" Dylan asked.

"I don't know. I mean, don't take this the wrong way, but a lot of us always thought this would be you."

"Oh, why would I be offended by that?" Dylan asked, clearly annoyed.

"Listen, I'm sorry. Forget I said anything. It's just with the way you talk about everything, like your job and life in general. You would never do something like this though, would ya?"

"Seriously? Of course not? What do you mean, how I talk about stuff?"

"Oh hell, Dylan, I didn't mean anything by it. You've just gotten real negative in your old age….and I thought…forget I brought it up. OK?"

"Yeah, sure. Water under the bridge. I mean, you didn't mean anything by it, why should I care."

"Sweet. Thanks man," Jim said, clearly not picking up on his tone. "Hey, speaking of crazy people from our past; what's up with John these days?"

"Oh, you know, drunk and crazy like always. He's actually passed out outside. Want to go fuck with him?"

"Yes, Dylan, yes I do," Jim said and grabbed a sharpie from off the counter and followed Dylan outside.

In the two years David Estern had been on death row, parts of his mind were lost, never to be found again. A part of him had already died. He felt like he was in a submarine that hadn't come up to the surface in ages. He was detached, isolated, alone. He thought about death all of the time. He welcomed it.

During the trial, he had denied counsel from the very beginning. He pled no contest and after being sentenced to death had made it a point to drop his appeals. The part of his mind that made him feel empathy, sorrow and guilt had returned almost immediately after he committed his crime, and it ate away at him from the inside like bacteria.

He said very little during the trial about why he did it other than "It had to be done." Recently a prison psychologist, Lawrence Thompson, had pried some shocking information out of him, a detail he was too afraid to admit before. David had told Lawrence that he had heard voices, one voice anyway. This voice commanded him to do what he did. David told Lawrence that, although the voice had gone away some time ago, he knew that after he died he would meet the person who the voice belonged to. After hearing this, Lawrence Thompson set off on a last-second plea deal to save David Estern's life. There seemed to be no stopping his crusade to do so.

That same voice, however, would soon tell Lawrence to do the exact opposite.

Dylan was letting John sleep as he closed up the store. He had not budged while Jim had written "Dick Bag" in block letters on his forehead with magic marker. After debating whether they should try to get him to pee his pants by sticking his hand in warm water, Jim had gotten a call from his girlfriend and had to leave. Dylan didn't see the point in waking him, as he was enjoying the silence.

He was lost deep in thought, wondering if he really did want to get chicken wings at Reever's with John or if he wanted a burrito and a margarita from Chubby's. He couldn't remember if John was allowed back in Chubby's because of the Enchilada incident of '04 when John threw a beef and cheese enchilada at a pair of passing Mormons, knocking them off their ten speeds.

Dylan was counting the money in the register for the day when he looked outside and saw her. The girl he had been waiting for all day. "John!" he screamed. "Wake up man, she's here, she's here!" Dylan ran out the door, knocked over a display case, leapt over the railing of the Outer Shell and ran towards the Line. He ran down the hill towards the line of forty or so travelers and stopped just short of them. He realized he had never been this close to them before, and a feeling of uneasiness washed across his body. It was the same feeling he had when he attended his Grandfather's funeral a few years earlier and he stood before his open casket. Death always had a way of making the living feel uneasy.

He was just ahead of the girl, and he figured, since he made it this far, he might as well give it a shot. "Hi! Fancy seeing you here," Dylan said with a nervous crack in his voice. The girl remained stoic, looking straight ahead and not breaking stride. "I'm Dylan, I uh, I don't know what I'm doing. I just...can you hear me?" The girl failed to acknowledge his presence and continued to walk forward. Dylan followed her stride for stride, thinking of the next brilliant thing to say. He looked up and realized the Outer Shell was getting smaller and smaller, as he was now about 100 yards away from where he started talking to her.

"Look, if you could just tell me your name, that would be a start," he continued. "I'm not trying to bother you and ask you a bunch of questions like I'm sure everyone does. I just want to get to know you. Maybe it would make these little visits of yours a little more pleasurable, ya know, if you had someone to talk to."

The girl remained silent as Dylan kept stride with her for a few more paces. Dejected and hurt, Dylan realized the Line was nearly in the woods and decided walking into a dark forest with a bunch of dead people wasn't something he wanted to do. "Well, this is my stop," Dylan joked. "See ya next time, I guess?" Although the girl continued to look forward, Dylan swore he saw a small smile form on her lips.

Shocked, Dylan stopped in his tracks as the girl and the rest of her line disappeared into the dark trees. "I saw that!" Dylan screamed at her as she walked away. "Didn't I?" he thought.

He walked back in the direction he came from and felt slightly satisfied. She had clearly given him a sign. She wanted to talk to him but couldn't for some reason. As he approached the Outer Shell, he saw John leaning on the railing smoking a cigarette. "Well?" John asked.

Dylan just gave a quick smile and shrugged his shoulders not knowing if he should tell him what he had thought just happened. "It's a start I guess."

Chapter 7

"And in conclusion," Mr. Black continued, while the Devil paced menacingly behind him, "we again would just like to congratulate everyone for doing an incredible job. We're running a real tight ship down here, and we're hoping this excellence will continue into the next year. Now, as I promised, the Devil himself would like to say a few words," Mr. Black then prompted the room to applaud as he came forward ready to address his staff.

The Devil was extremely disappointing when compared to the usual depiction of him. He was not at all like the Jacob Epstein's famous statue or even Tim Curry's depiction of him in Legend. He was not a massive, hulking force littered with sinewy muscles, gnashing teeth and bull-like horns. He was frail, malnourished and horribly pale. He dressed like a combination of Eddie Munster and Evel Knievel. A stereotypical goth kid, locked in the eternal parent's basement that was his section of the underworld.

His accent, sometimes tough to decipher, was said to be a combination of all of the accents in human history, which could be most closely mimicked by a person from New England sucking on a bag of marbles. He claimed to be able to speak and understand all of the languages in the world except Icelandic. Also, his Spanish was surprisingly poor. This was commonplace with most Devils – a tenuous grasp on multiple languages, but a master at none, making day-to-day conversations confusing and humorous.

This particular devil, although widely regarded by the people in his region of Hell as *The Devil,* was far from the only one. As people had found early on, there were multiple exits and nearly as many devils. Hundreds of thousands of people die every day, and a good portion of them go to Hell. It is unreasonable to think that one entity could hold dominion over them all. Under the United States alone there are 65 Devils. This is attributed to a largely Judeo-Christian belief structure and an overwhelming number of living assholes.

The Jersey Devil (yes, like the Hockey team) was officially titled DVL03US but preferred to be called Daman because Damien and Damion were already been spoken for by DVL01 and DVL02, respectfully. DVL03US, Daman, watched over and under all of New Jersey and some of Northern Pennsylvania – the non-Amish parts.

Daman thought he did a great job running his particular segment of the underworld, but he would soon find out he was pretty much the only one that thought that.

Strutting towards his disciples, Daman let out a wide, uncharacteristic smile. "Mah friends," he began "I wood jus like to congradulate everyone for doing such a bang oop job. We're rahning a real tight sheep around here and we're hoping this excellence will continue into dye next yare. Dis is da year of da Devil…and for Hell, and we will always…"
The room sat in silence waiting for Daman to continue.
"Be good. Dat's it, great meeting, you can leave."

Speeches like this were pretty common for Daman. He would start strong, having a plan in his head of what he wanted to say. The first half he would repeat what Neville had already said, and then half-way through he would usually sputter out, completely losing his train of thought and leaving a room full of confused people.
Jay Stevenson and his "co-workers" all left the room to return to their highly important positions, leaving only Daman and Mr. Black in the room.

"Great speech sir, I think you really wowed them," Neville said.

"Thank you, Neville. I was terrifying?"

"Yes sir," Neville answered. "Extremely."

"I feel lahk I need to make beeger produchon out of eet…maybe mor flames?"

"I think that's a brilliant idea," said a voice with a thick, English accent coming from the shadows. "While I have you, perhaps we can discuss some further matters.

Daman and Neville turned towards the voice and saw Gregory Irons sitting motionless in a seat at the back of the room.

"Mr. Irons," Neville said startled. "I'm very sorry, I thought everyone had left."

"No bother to apologize," Irons said rising from his chair. "I was hoping to catch both of you. There's something that needs to be addressed."

"Addressed?" Daman said quizzically. "I though we cavered everyting?"

"This is one of those big picture things, Old boy," Irons said, rising from his seat and approaching the two.

Daman was widely regarded as the figurehead of Hell, and Mr. Black was indeed his right hand man, but many felt that it was Gregory Irons who actually ran things. Irons rose through the ranks quickly using a mixture of fear and intimidation. He had a reputation for being ruthless, which is something that the Devil could never obtain no matter how hard he tried. Guards lowered their heads when he walked by, Inhabitants shook with fear and Daman and Mr. Black pretty much let him do anything he wanted to do. Because of his nature and the harsh penalties and tortures he was always instituting, he had earned a nickname: the Dragon. The Dragon's personality seemed like the real deal to those around him, but, in actuality, what no one in the underworld knew is that

Gregory Iron's entire personality was an act. He was not, as everyone thought him to be, a former London Homicide detective gone bad, but actually a scared but imaginative introvert from Middlebrook, New Jersey, named Steven Arby.

As a child, Steven was always lost in a world of fantasy. Dungeons and Dragons and HP Lovecraft Japanimation all played a part in his upbringing. He immersed himself in the culture and spent hours in his room reading, collecting cards and plotting his next quest in D&D. If you're guessing that because of this he did not have a lot of friends, you would be correct. If you're thinking all of this sounds like a great way for a teen to spend his formative years, then you are probably very similar to Steven and should leave your house and go outside for some fresh air.

Even though he had acquaintances that he played the game with, other than when they were battling Orc forces, or traversing across an icy tundra to rescue a princess, he still had a hard time relating to them. While the game was going, he was in his element. Every character was fleshed out, complete with voices, attributes and back stories, and he would act out each character with fervor and candor. Once the game was over, he went back to being shy and awkward, even with other nerds. He would remain this way going into high school, which inevitably lead to bullying. Nothing too horrific, just enough for Steven to once again feel out of place and left out.

He would go on to attend college at Montclair State University, where he studied Theatre. With it came a group of fellow students who, like him, had a penchant for fantasy, mystery and talking in funny accents pretty much all of the time. His first year of college was the happiest in Steven's life. However, because of Steven's mind having a tendency to wander, he spent too much time watching Monty Python and film noir and failed every class his first semester.

He returned to Middlebrook dejected, disappointed and miserable.
Out of options, he took a job at Video One, a local video rental
store and began what would be, unbeknownst to him, the last year
of his life. The video store once again offered solace from the
outside world as he perused the store's Science Fiction section and,
between customers, lost himself in the world of Dune, The Dark
Crystal and The Dungeons and Dragons movie that, while
considered horrible by nearly every critic, was one of Steven's
personal favorites. He had memorized every line uttered by
Profion, played by the usually great Jeremy Irons. It is here he also
developed an affinity for Guy Ritchie movies and fell in love with
the charismatic and colorful villains he created. He would quote
these villains when no one was in the store, working on his English
accent and dreaming of the day he could return to Montclair and
impress all of his former classmates with what he had learned
about being a sinister English villain.

It was during Steven's 34th viewing of The Dungeons and Dragons
movie that the first robbery occurred. It was 11:45 p.m., and
Steven was getting set to close up the store when they came in.
Three men in masks holding large knives came in and demanded
the money from the register and the safe. Having no allegiance to
the store's owners, he complied without a fight. The men, seeing
how easy this was the first time, came back again and again and
again. After each successful robbery, Steven's boss would berate
him for his cowardice and demand that he stand up to these men
and protect the store. "…there's a gun below the counter. For
Christ's sake, use it!" Four times in a row, Steven did nothing. On
their fifth and final visit, one of the men mocked Steven as he left.
"See you next time, Bronson," an obvious dig at his lack of
backbone. It was this remark, along with an entire life of being

picked on, that convinced Steven that he had had enough.

As the last man turned his back on him and followed his snickering friends out of the store, Steven reached below the counter, pulled out the desert eagle stashed below the now empty register, aimed at the back of the closest head he saw and fired. Like a helium balloon meeting a pin, the robbers head exploded, shooting blood and membrane all over the 99 cent VHS bin. The two men in front of him jumped in astonishment and then froze in fear as they looked back at Steven holding the smoking gun, his eyes wide and his knuckles white on the gun's ivory grip. Steven, unflinching, squeezed the trigger twice more, dropping the other two robbers to the floor.

At that moment, something washed over Steven, and he, like he had so many times in the past, become someone else. "If the milk turns out to be sour, I ain't the kinda pussy to drink it," he said quietly to himself in a practiced English accent. "Fucking cunts." All of those years of being picked on and disenchanted had lead Steven Arby to want to be someone else. Now he had shocked himself into being just that. He was a combination of every bad English villain he had watched and read about. The only thing that remained of Steven Arby was a desire to exact revenge on a world that had repeatedly kicked him around. He walked out of the store, gun in hand, and shot and killed three more people, squeezing off each round with an icy glare and a clever line spoken in a bad English accent.

When a barrage of cop cars showed up minutes later and demanded he drop his weapon, Steven raised his arms to the sky and shouted "I will rain fire on you from the sky," just like Jeremy Irons did in Dungeons and Dragons. Officer Jeremy Rowe fired one shot, hitting Steven in the temple and killing him instantly. He was cast naked into the underworld, and a group of guards descended upon him hoping to put the usual scare into a new arrival. The new version of Steven Arby leapt to his feet, grabbed the nearest guard and put him in a tight headlock. The guard gasped for air as Steven said, "You don't like that, do you boy? Good. I can use every ounce of your anguish." The other guards were astonished at this, never seeing an arrival like this before. It was at that moment that the Dragon was born. Steven Arby, with his fake English accent, told the crowd his name was Gregory Irons and that he was going to be in charge now. No one ever checked to see if Steven's origins were accurate. They were all too afraid and, well, Hell is just a very poorly run organization. Gregory Irons knew this, and he had made it his mission ever since to change the culture of the underworld and to continue to carry out his revenge on the world that had started that night at the video store.

Here in the conference room with the Devil and Neville Black he continued his plan. "Things need to bloody well change," Irons said.

"What changes?" Neville asked. "We just had a whole meeting about how everything was running smoothly."

"We did not. *You* did. Some of us feel you run this place like bloody Disneyland and not the horrifying place it's supposed to be. Where's the blood, me mateys?"

"Diznee land?" Daman asked turning towards Neville.

"Yes sir, you know, Mickey Mouse. You love him."

"Ah yes." Daman's eyes widened in delight. "Mee Kee."

"The Inhabitants walk around like they're on holiday," Irons continued. "We need to make them fear us more. We need to break their spirit further. We need to spill more blood than ever before. We need to make this Hell a little more...."

"Fun?" Daman interrupted.

"Hellish."

"Well what do you suggest?" Neville asked.

"I have some ideas," Irons said with a menacing smile. "We need more blokes like me, or people like us, to arrive here."

"Well, how do we do that?" Neville asked? "We have no control over who comes here."

"Oh, I just have a feeling they're on their way. I've been waiting for years for some of them."

Chapter 8

"Hey, Estern, you hungry?" David Estern turned to see William Gold, the newest civilian volunteer at the Death Row unit standing at the front of his cell holding a tray in front of him.

Estern was being held in an experimental wing of Grant Park Penitentiary called The PHP Project, short for People Helping Prisoners. Due to cutbacks, the prison had decided to enlist the help of a local church, asking volunteers to come into Death Row and feed the prisoners, clean up after them and, David's least favorite part of the program, talk to them about God. The volunteers had helped to decorate the cell area, making it look like the lobby of a stuffy church. It was supposed to help the prisoners feel at ease, but David felt it only made him feel crazier. "William. Hello, yes I am," he said to the visibly nervous volunteer.

He walked over to the heavy metal door and retrieved the tray from Gold through a small opening at his waist, giving him a forced smile before retreating to his tiny dinner table to begin eating. An actual guard remained disinterested at a nearby desk, checking his Friendster account.

David turned his back to the volunteer, sat at the tiny table in his cell and began eating.

"You're not gonna say grace?" Gold asked him. "Even in your…situation?"

"I never was a God-fearing man," Estern responded with his mouth half-full of food. "I guess I just don't see the point of starting now."

"But aren't you afraid? You done some bad things, David, and you need to repent for them. Before they shoot that stuff into ya you'll have to make peace with the Lord or, well, who knows where you're gonna end up."

David stopped chewing for a second and looked sternly at Gold.

"I know exactly where I'm gonna end up."

"Where? Why?"

David stopped chewing and looked at William, "He told me exactly where I am going. He said I had to do it. It's all part of his plan."

"What plan? Who told you?"

"The man I've been talking to William: The Dragon."

Chapter 9

"Cataloop. Cataloop. Cataloop." Dylan had been listening to his mom, Grace, attempt to say the word caterpillar for several minutes now and "cataloop" was the closest she had gotten.

"She was better at it last time. Is she getting worse?" He asked the pathologist, Lilly.

"Nah Ginning wese," Grace said

"Write what you're trying to say, dear," Lilly said to Grace, sliding over a black magic marker and spiral notebook.

"Aaaah" she responded in frustration sliding the book back across the table.

"OK Grace, I'm sorry. I understand it's been a frustrating day." Lilly said. "Dylan, let's take a walk. We'll be right back, Grace." Grace waved a dismissive hand at them, turning towards an outside facing window. Lilly motioned for Dylan to follow her out of the room and into the hallway. Dylan followed her and shut the door behind him.

"You shouldn't say that stuff in front of your mom," she said. "It doesn't help her."

"Well, what do you want me to say? She's not a baby, she should know if she's getting worse. I mean how many more years of this do we have to go through this before she's better?"

"We don't know if she'll ever get better Dylan. We can only keep trying and hope that her speech improves with each session. In the meantime, she needs your constant encouragement. Dylan, I've told you before that's pretty much all you can do for her – be supportive and encouraging. There's no way to fix this, you have to accept that."

The two of them had had this conversation before and it never seemed to stick with him. The fact that his mother was "unfixable" was something he would never accept.

Lilly extended a reassuring hand and rested it on Dylan's shoulder. "I'm here for you Dylan. Always remember that."

Dylan looked at her and her chestnut hair and ocean green eyes and wished all woman treated him this nice, "You want to have a drink with me tonight?"

"Oh, Dylan. Not again?"

"What? Am I really that bad that you won't go out to have one drink with me?"

"No Dylan, you are a very nice guy, and I'm sure a lot of woman would love to have a drink with you and, while I am flattered, I just don't think it's appropriate. We've gone over this before."

"I know. I know. I get it. You can't blame me for trying can you?"

"Sure I can," Lilly said with a smile, "but I'll let you off the hook this one last time, just try to remember this conversation next time you come in, OK?"

"Sounds good," Dylan said.

She smiled at him and reentered the room where Grace was. Dylan rolled his eyes and felt embarrassed that it had happened again. He looked at his watch and saw that it was almost 5:00. He had told John he would pick him up at 5:30 to get an early start at the bar. He knew that the only way to truly erase what had just happened was to get very, very drunk.

After sitting in on his mother's speech therapy sessions, Dylan usually found it best to unwind at a local bar. Dylan's version of unwinding usually entailed eating a lot of greasy food and drinking enough beer and whiskey that he forgot about how upset his mother's affliction made him.

Dylan picked up John in his 1983 rust-green Subaru and drove straight to Reevers, a bar with cheap alcohol that was an almost equal stumbling distance between their apartments. Reevers was your typical college hangout, but for people who had never been to college or hadn't been in a very long time. Various sports memorabilia hung haphazardly around the wooden interior while twenty-something bartenders in Giants jerseys poured shots of Sloppy Pussy and Surfer on Acid for listless dropouts who were all trying to fuck each other, but would most likely go home alone. Dylan hated Reevers but somehow still ended up hanging out there four to five nights per week. He was currently in the process of poking at a freshly devoured chicken wing bone and telling a mildly interested John about his encounter with the dead girl from the Line.

"So she smiled at ya, huh?" John playfully asked Dylan while wiping wing sauce off his face.

"Dude, believe me if you want, but I know what I saw. It was a smile, maybe a slight wink too."

"Ooooh, you didn't mention the wink, Dylan! A wink changes everything! Did she give you a hand job too?"

"No, but your girlfriend did last night," Dylan retorted playfully, throwing a meatless chicken wing bone at his friend.

"Not possible dude," John said. "Jenelle was with me last night."

"Are you sure about that?" Dylan asked. "I thought you couldn't remember anything that happened with her."

"I'm pretty sure she was there last night…"John said before pausing to recollect his latest bout of binge drinking. "Regardless, at least my girlfriend is a real person and not a corpse. What exactly is your plan with this girl anyway?"

"I told you I don't have one," Dylan said. "I'm just kinda talking…maybe she's listening."

"Well I think it all sounds great, Dylan. You're gonna get a dead girl to fall in love with you, buy a nice little home in the suburbs and praise her master and lord Satan before being sodomized by wizards every night!"

"Wizards?" Dylan asked.

"Oh I'm sure the Devil has wizards working for him. All that black magic they practice, someone had to teach them that shit."

"You're right man, I never thought about it that way," Dylan responded. "Your theories are really air-tight, buddy. Way to go. Wizards. Brilliant."

"Thank you sir," John said tipping his beer bottle towards his friend and finishing the bottle in one long gulp.

"You're getting pretty wasted tonight, huh," Dylan noticed. "What's the occasion?"

"Janelle called earlier. She said she got some sexy underwear. I'm supposed to go over there after this and, I just don't think I can go into that situation dry. I need some backup."

"Gotcha." Dylan said shaking his head in disbelief. "Want to do a shot of booze then?"

"Now you're talking, buddy. This rounds on me."

John wearily stood up, and swayed back and forth while checking the contents of his wallet, eventually pulling out four crumpled dollar bills. "Loan me a five? I want to get a beer too."

Perplexed, but in no mood to fight with his drunk friend, Dylan handed him a five-dollar bill.

"Thanks. Jager bomb?"

"You know I don't drink that shit," Dylan said.

"Yeah, me neither. Black Zinfandel!" John said and walked off towards the bar.

Dylan sometimes wondered why he hung out with John so much. He was usually drunk, which usually got them into trouble. They had been banned from almost every bar in the Brinton area. John and Dylan had grown up together and, although he loved him like a brother, sometimes he wondered why he couldn't seem to shake him. He started to realize that John was an inevitable factor in his life, like death and taxes. He would always be around and he would never change. Despite the constant amount of bullshit that John brought into his life, he knew deep down that he would do anything for him, despite the very, very limited skills he had to offer.

Without his friend sitting across from him to amuse him, Dylan began surveying the other patrons in the bar. It was filled with a sea of faces that he recognized, but could not put any names to them. He looked over at a couple playing Golden Tee and was pretty sure they both worked at Wegmans, the grocery store close to the gift shop that he would walk to for lunch and cigarettes. He thought maybe he had talked to the male about the Nets trading for Vince Carter once, but he wasn't sure.

There were a few people that he had gone to high school with sitting at a table towards the bathrooms, including Stephanie Lowell, who he had once made out with at a party. If they passed by him, he would say hi, but they were too far away and Dylan had a shot coming his way if John ever stumbled back.

Then, sitting at the bar, nursing a beer, Dylan saw a man he was sure he recognized, but he just couldn't place from where. He didn't look like the typical Reevers regular, but Dylan was sure he recognized him. He stared intently at his face trying to place him somewhere in his memory. He was a black man, in his mid to late 30s wearing a white t-shirt and blue jeans. The thing that caught Dylan's attention was his hair cut. The man was sporting a mid-90s era flat top sticking up about four inches off the top of his head. Dylan had seen this haircut before and not just in rap videos. Just when Dylan was about to make the connection, John came stumbling back and was yelling at someone across the bar. "Yeah, you will see me later. You pick the parking lot and I'll be there, bitch!" John then turned to Dylan and said in a quieter voice, "I'm not gonna be there. That dude would fucking kill me."

Dylan saw that John had only one beer and one shot in his hands. Assuming he already drank his, Dylan waited a few moments for John to bestow the sweet, brown liquid on him. Instead, John downed it in one gulp, chasing it with a long swig of beer. Dylan glared at him with daggers in his eyes.

"What?" John asked perplexed. "Did you want one too?"

"Never mind," he said. "Look at that guy over there sitting at the bar. Does he look familiar to you?"

John squinted hard in the direction of the man for several moments.

"Yeah," he finally said. "He works at Wegmans."

"No, not that guy, THAT guy right fucking there!" Dylan yelled out and pointed emphatically at the man at the bar. He had yelled loud enough for a few bar patrons to turn around in the direction of the two, including the man in question who noticed that Dylan was now pointing at him. He awkwardly turned away but not before John had a good enough look at him to figure out who it was.

"He looks like the dude from the Line. The guy I can't be friends with, cause it's racist. The Play."

"I literally have no idea what you are talking about…" Before Dylan could finish his sentence, he suddenly knew what his drunk friend was rambling about. The man they were looking at right now, who was casually enjoying a drink at a bar, was the man they had seen earlier today, walking in a Line protruding from what was presumed to be the mouth of Hell – the man they called The Kid.

"He still looks cool," John said.

The Kid, seeing that the two drunk men at the table seemed to be yelling at each other and pointing wildly at him, decided it was time for him to go, so he threw some money down for the beer and decided to make his exit.

"He's leaving, man," Dylan noticed. "We gotta follow him!"

"Follow who?" John asked, hiccupping on his last word.

"Gaaah," Dylan screamed in exasperation and walked quickly towards the door with the man from the bar just closing the door behind him. Dylan opened the door and surveyed the parking lot. Initially it seemed empty as Dylan listened for movement in the calm air. He heard the beep of a car being opened, turned and saw The Kid pointing his automatic opener at a car across the parking lot, trying to elude Dylan as he was clearly frightened.

"Excuse me!" Dylan yelled at him. The man did not turn around, quickening his pace and pressing harder on his car opener.

"Sir," Dylan continued. "I just want to ask you a couple questions. Please slow down." The man started in a half jog towards his car. Dylan, not wanting to let this man get away, began sprinting like a mad man towards him.

"Would you slow down for fucks sake! I just want to talk to you!" The man finally turned around and saw Dylan running at full speed towards him.

"Stay back, I have a gun!" he said while reaching inside of his coat as one usually does when they are searching for a weapon.

Hearing this and not wanting to get shot, Dylan tried to stop running towards him. Unable to slow down he barreled full force into the man, knocking him to the concrete and landing on top of him. Now on the ground, the man, who thought that Dylan had tackled him on purpose, wrestled around and tried to free himself from under Dylan.

"I'll shoot you!" the man screamed. "I have a gun! Help!"

"I just want to talk to you!" Dylan yelled back. "Calm down!"

"Then why did you tackle me?!"

"I didn't mean to! Relax!"

"What kind of awkward klutz tackles people by accident!?"

Dylan then managed to out-muscle his opponent so he had a firm grasp on both his arms, making it nearly impossible for the man to move them. Realizing his assailant had the upper hand, the man stopped squirming and looked up at Dylan.

"I don't have a gun," the man said calmly. "I was just trying to scare you."

"I'm really not trying to hurt you," Dylan responded, "I just want to talk."

"Yeah, I guess I heard you say that. Please get off of me. Your knee is crushing my balls."

"Oh shit! Yeah, sorry." Dylan got off the man and grabbed him by the hand, helping him to his feet. "I'm really sorry man," Dylan began. "This has obviously gotten way out of hand. Come back in the bar and let me buy you a drink. We'll sort this whole thing out."

"About what?! What the hell is this all about?!"

"I'll explain everything, just please come back inside. No tackling, I promise."

"Your nose is bleeding, dude," the man said to Dylan. Dylan wiped his fingers below his nostrils and saw the now familiar sight of blood. It was only a little, it had been much worse.

"Yeah, it's cool, it happens. So will you come inside with me, please?"

"Two drinks. And some Jalapeno poppers. Then I'll come inside."

"Deal," Dylan said.

The two men walked side by side back into Reevers. The man was wondering if this was a good idea but justified that a crowded bar was a better setting to talk to a lunatic than an empty parking lot.

Dylan, now certain that this was indeed The Kid, was wondering what type of drink he should buy for a dead man.

Chapter 10

Lauren knew the walk very well at this point. She could do it with her eyes closed, and she often did. The travelers had become trail-burned like old horses at a tourist ranch.

She knew that she was about halfway done with the walk at this point and had about another four miles before she was back at the entrance. She was going to try and breathe in as much fresh air as she could.

She hoped no one had seen her smile at the guy from the gift shop. She was sure she had done it sly enough, but, after he broadcast it for the rest of the world to hear, she worried that he might have given her away. She braced herself for the inevitable lashing from a nearby guard, who marched in the line with the rest of them in an undercover fashion. She relaxed a little, knowing that had a guard seen this happen, retribution would have been almost immediate, and, since none of them had hopped out of line yet, she rationalized that she was in the clear.

Who the hell was that guy, and why was he trying to talk to her? Was he that desperate to try to get laid? She worried that if he kept this up he would get her into serious trouble one day. She also thought maybe in some way he could help her. Maybe even get her out of her current situation.

She decided not to think about it any further and focus on the remainder of the walk. It was a beautiful day and she wanted to soak all of it in. She'd be "home" soon enough.

The first few hours back in Hell were always the most depressing for any traveler. After a visit to the surface, everything there just seemed so much worse. The neon track lighting that was hung all over the ceilings always seemed to be a little brighter and nauseating, the screams were a little louder and the numbing hopelessness that hung in the air seemed to permeate the pores. After breathing in the fresh air of the surface, the indefiniteness of Hell seemed to become a little more permanent.

Lauren sometimes wondered why she left at all. After returning to the underworld, Lauren had gone to her sleeping quarters for a few minutes to rest and then realized she had to get up and head right back out to meet with counselor Stevenson. She was again standing in line at the counselor's office like she had done many times before, only this time, she was waiting to have her post surface follow up, in which Inhabitants had to answer a few questions about how their time on the surface went and in what ways their experience could improve.

Lauren thought these meetings were the most worthless of all as, even when valid concerns were given, nothing ever changed. She was nervous about this particular meeting, though, and hoped that her brief encounter with the gift-shop employee would go unnoticed.

"Well," a voice said behind her. "How was it?"

"Just fine, Artie," Lauren responded, recognizing the voice.

"I had a nice visit too, thanks for asking," he began. "I was about five people behind you in the Line so I got to see you pretty much the whole time. I'm hoping one day I get to walk right behind you. That would make the view so, so, much better."

Lauren rolled her eyes and held back a little vomit when thinking about someone as disgusting as Artie staring at her ass for miles.

"So who is the guy?" Artie then asked.

Lauren turned in surprise, knowing exactly what he meant, but did not want to admit she did.

"What guy?" she asked in mock confusion.

"Oh you know, the guy who leapt over the railing of the store when he saw you, the guy who followed you for nearly a mile and the guy who seemed like he had talked to you before. Friend of yours? You know you're not supposed to talk to anyone when you're up there."

"I know, Artie. I know and I didn't. He talked to me and I said nothing back. Want to see how good I am at it?"

"I'd be careful if I were you, missy. I know people."

Lauren then turned her back to Artie with no intentions of saying a word to him ever again. Regardless, she was worried.

Lauren was going to take the offensive on her interview with counselor Stevenson. She was simply going to tell him about the encounter with the gift-shop employee and explain how he tried to talk to her, but she did not respond at all. That kind of thing happened all of the time, especially in the early days, after the Exit was discovered. Tons of people would run up and ask people questions, and, if a traveler didn't respond, they would actually be rewarded. Lauren was hoping this would be the case this time. Man, she really wished that idiot hadn't yelled at her. She had gotten through the line and was now sitting in front of counselor Stevenson, waiting for the usual line of questions.

"Okay, Lauren," the counselor began. "So, back from the big upstairs, huh? You enjoy it?"

"Yeah, I did. Thanks"

"Good. Well, I just need to ask a few questions as per usual. You ready?

"Sure."

"Rate your experience on a scale of one to ten with ten being very pleasurable, one being not pleasurable and five being somewhat pleasurable."

"Umm, five, I guess."

"Somewhat pleasurable, huh? Okay, good," the counselor responded, not seeming to pay attention to Lauren's answer at all. "Rate the staff, me included, that you dealt with in this experience with one being not efficient, ten being efficient and five being somewhat efficient."

Although Lauren hated everything about Hell, she still felt a little sorry for the counselor and, not wanting to hurt his feelings, she responded with a ten.

"Ahhh, great, super. OK, Lauren, the last question is: Did you have any contact with the living during your visit to the surface?"

Lauren paused for a second and then responded, "No. Well...yes. Well, I mean, someone tried to talk to me, but I didn't respond. Some guy."

"Some guy, you say? Had you had prior contact with this person before?"

"No."

"Well, OK, we'll talk with the Line officers and see if any of them witnessed the incident. It doesn't sound serious, though. These things happen. We'll do a quick review, and, if we deem that no actions are needed, we'll most likely reward you for your actions. Do you understand that?"

"I do. Thanks Mr. Stevenson."

"You're welcome, Lauren. That will be all."

Lauren stood up and walked towards the door. Just as she was about to exit, the counselor called to her. "Oh Lauren, one more thing."

"Yes."

"Call me Jay," he smiled and gave her a thumbs up.

Chapter 11

Dylan, John and The Kid all sat at the table in awkward silence. After convincing the man to come back into Reevers with him, Dylan realized he didn't know what to say to the man. Initially they made conversation about the drinks they had chosen, but that had come to an abrupt halt after John exclaimed "whiskey makes me fuck better."

Dylan had so many questions to ask him, but, after the way their initial meeting had gone, he didn't want to be too aggressive and scare him off.

The Kid told them his real name was Chris and that he was originally from Buffalo but had moved into the area after high school to be closer to New York City.

Dylan of course didn't care about any of this. He wanted to know why this man, who was last seen walking out of the Exit from the underworld was now in front of him sipping a gin and tonic at a crappy neighborhood bar. Dylan was racking his brain trying to find the appropriate line of questioning when John blurted out, "So what are you?"

Normally, John's forwardness upset Dylan but he couldn't think of a better way to get this conversation going.

"What am I?" Chris asked. "I'm not sure I follow you? Like what do I do for a living?"

"Sure," Dylan said. "Let's start there. What do you do for a living?"

"Oh, odds and ends here and there. I do some freelancing for a few different magazines. I want to be a writer," Chris responded.

"You mean, wanted to be a writer, right?" Dylan prompted.

"Nooooo," Chris said slowly. "I still want to be one. I don't think it's out of the realm of possibility just yet."

"Even in Hell?" John burped out.

"Hell?" Chris asked. "What in the world are you..."

In midsentence, Chris stopped and finally realized what the two lunatics were getting at.

"Ooooh," he chuckled. "Ya know, boys, if you have questions you want to ask me, just go ahead and ask them. It would have saved us a whole lot of trouble, and that whole episode in the parking lot could have gone much smoother."

Dylan didn't want to waste time any longer. He leaned forward and put his palms on the table. "Are you the guy we keep seeing in the Line coming out of Hell?" Dylan asked intently. "Are you one of them, ya know, dead?"

"Yes and no," Chris responded.

"What does that mean?" Dylan asked.

"Yes, there is a chance you may have seen me walking around with a bunch of dead people, but, no, I am not dead.

"Then what's the story there?" Dylan asked. "How do you do it?"

"Let's see, this must have been a few days ago when you last saw me, right? Oh man, where to begin? I guess it started when I lost my last job," he began. "If you want to know more about it, I'll tell you, but we may be here awhile."

Dylan turned to the bartender, whistled and held up three fingers for the bartender to bring them three more drinks. He would listen for as long as it took.

Chris had been telling him his secrets about walking the Line with the dead for about a half-hour now. After giving them a brief history into why he had decided to do this in the first place, he went on to tell them about all of his trials and errors and had just told them the biggest key to it all.

"So let me get this straight," Dylan said, still puzzled by what Chris had just told him. "The key to staying in the Line is being sad?"

"Pretty much," Chris responded. "Getting into the Line in the first place is actually pretty easy, but staying there is a whole different thing. You have to carry yourself a certain way. You have to act sort of hopeless. That's how I got in the Line in the first place. I had just been laid off from the newspaper I was working at, and I just felt like shit. It's like it was calling to me. I don't even remember how it really happened, but I never made it all the way to the end. I never have. It's like I'm not hopeless enough."

"That should be no problem for this sad sack," John said, pointing a half empty beer bottle at Dylan. "This dude is always sad. That's why we call him Eeyore."

"Who calls me Eeyore?" Dylan asked.

"Everyone, dude," John responded.

"Whatever," Dylan said, realizing they were getting too far off of the important topic. He needed to know more from Chris.

"Can you just," Dylan began, "start from the beginning?"

"OK," Chris began, "This was maybe, two or three years ago. Like I said, I had just gotten laid off, budget cut back or something, from *The Daily Sentinel*. I had gone off into the woods by that gift shop you work at with a bottle of whiskey, and I was just sitting, drinking and feeling sorry for myself. Then I saw them coming towards me. Just dead souls, marching off towards the bowels of Hell, devoid of hope. It sounds weird, but, for the first time in a while, I understood their pain. I watched them for awhile and then I remember feeling real dizzy, and the next thing I knew I was staring at a head in front of me. I was walking with the dead people. By the time I realized what I was doing, it seemed like I was right back out again, off in the woods somewhere. I still do it from time to time, but I never make it very far.

"You just walked right in Line with them," John asked, "just like that?"

"I guess I sort of eased into it," Chris explained. "I got closer and closer to the Line and learned the cadence of it. I figured out the pulse of it. I felt its pain. I seem to stay in Line for less time these days. Last time you saw me I got booted out pretty quickly. I must be happier these days."

Dylan was starting to think this guy was a complete nut and maybe everything he was saying was a lie, but he had seen him there. He had to be telling the truth.

"I also learned that not everyone there is marching. Some people are watching."

"Watching?" Dylan asked.

"Yeah, I still haven't figured out what they are, guards or something. I first saw this when someone tried to step out of Line, and one of the Watchers came over and dragged them back in. Luckily, at the time, I was still a long way away from the Line."

"How can you tell which ones are the Watchers?" Dylan asked.

"From up close," Chris said. "It's their eyes. Travelers' eyes are completely lifeless and dead. They're always looking straight forward. Watcher's eyes are shifty and always moving. They're always looking for something."

"That makes sense," Dylan said, "but how can you tell that from far away? What if you get too close and it's too late?"

"Well, as I found out the hard way, if the Watchers catch you, they'll beat the shit out of you. They are big dudes, and they always have weapons: tazers, clubs, you name it."

"Gotta keep the riff raff out somehow," Dylan said.

"Exactly," Chris responded, "but even the times I didn't get caught, the Line would sense my presence and kick me out. It's like it's got a soul or something. It's hard to explain. You can trick it into thinking you're one of them, but not for very long."

"Can you show me?" Dylan asked.

"Show you? Why would I do that? I barely know you, and you just assaulted me in the parking lot about fifteen minutes ago."

"I don't know," Dylan said. "I mean, do you have anything better to do?"

Chris thought about this for a second.

"I guess not. Is tomorrow good for you?"

Chapter 12

Jay Stevenson heard a loud knock at his door. "Come in," he said as he straightened his posture and shuffled uncomfortably in his chair. The door creaked open and in walked Neville Black, methodically loping towards the counselor's desk.

"Mr. Stevenson," he said with a creepy grin pursing on his lips. "Not interrupting anything, am I?"

"No sir, please come in. Have a seat."

"I will in just a moment. I am not alone. Someone wants to speak with you."

"Here we go," thought the counselor, knowing what he was in store for. Smoke, fire, blah, blah, blah, guitars, "We Will Rock You," yadda, yadda, yadda, hail Satan and five minutes later the Devil was finally in the room.

"You may be seated," he said to counselor Stevenson, even though he had been in his chair the whole time.

"Have a seat, gentlemen," the counselor said to Mr. Black and Daman, motioning to two empty chairs in front of him. Mr. Black started towards one of the empty chairs before stopping in his tracks as Daman spoke. "We would prefer to stand, counselor," he began, causing Neville to move away from the chair back towards Daman, sidling up beside him like an attention-starved puppy. "For what I am about to tell you is of the utmost importance and will require much gesturing."

For all his posturing and grandstanding, Daman spoke at a very hushed volume that was sometimes difficult to hear. His tone was low and deliberate, like telling a ghost story around a campfire. It was slightly creepy overall, but in parts ridiculous and forced.

"I ask question," he began. "The Surface Passes. Why are you giving them to pretty much every mother and their sons." Daman had problems with common phrases.

"I suppose I don't turn a lot of people away," Jay began. "I just feel it makes it better for everyone down here. Inhabitants seem to behave better when they get to travel to the surface in the Line. I see no reason to deny anyone, really."

"People attend here for a reason," Daman said. "This is not a Disney Park. Do I look like Marky Mouse to you?" He said as he gazed menacingly at the counselor.

"It's Mickey sir," Neville said from behind him. "And, no, you don't. You're very terrifying."

"That's right," Daman agreed, "very terrifying." He paused for a second to let the sentiment set in before beginning again. "If this continues, the pass will become a ghost. A ghost with the chains and all of the carrying on and the haunting. Do I make myself clear?!"

"Ummm…" The counselor began before looking at Neville for further explanation.

"There have been some issues on the surface with some of our Travelers," Neville began. "It seems these issues have been escalating recently; Travelers trying to escape, talking to people on the surface, so on and so forth."

"We haven't had an escape in years, and they always come back. They have to." Jay said.

"This may be true, but it's only a matter of time before something major happens. We also feel this will cut back on the growing number of people who attempt to infiltrate the line and sneak down here for whatever reason." Neville said. "We feel that you need to be more selective with the people you give the passes to, people you feel won't step out of Line when they arrive on the surface. If this problem persists, we will shut down the program indefinitely."

"It turns to ghost," Daman demanded again.

"That's crazy," the counselor said. "You'd have a riot on your hands. The people would never stand for it. This is all they have."

"When the spirit is broken," Daman started, "the mind cannot function. If we have to break it all, we will do so." "Please counselor, do your job correctly and hopefully we will not have to resort to such drastic tactics. Do we understand each other?"

"Where is all of this coming from?" counselor Stevenson asked.

"Certain people have…urged us to change the way we do things around here. Now, these of course are merely suggestions, you understand. No one tells the Devil what to do, that's for sure. But we have taken these suggestions into consideration and feel that we do indeed want to follow them. We are asking all personnel to adhere to these rules or drastic measures may need to be taken. Do we make ourselves clear?"

"I suppose so," counselor Stevenson responded.

"Great," Mr. Black said condescendingly. "Now can you please dim the lights. The Devil is ready to make his exit."

Chapter 13

After their initial meeting at the bar, Dylan, Chris and John had agreed to meet at Dylan's apartment the following morning with hopes to survey the Line, learn all they could about it and attempt to infiltrate it.

Dylan had hardly slept the night before, thinking about the possibility of doing something he foolishly thought that no one had ever done before. He was sitting at his kitchen table, when his phone rang. "Hello?"

"Hado, Din," said his mother. It was not unusual for his mother to call him at strange times. Sometimes it was very early in the morning. Dylan knew that when the phone rang it was usually her, John or a wrong number.

"Hey ma," he began. "I really can't talk right now. I'm meeting some people here in a few minutes."

"Ah jes nee te teel," she said.

"What?"

"Ah jes nee te teel ya," she repeated. Dylan had gotten pretty good at deciphering a lot of his mom's jumbled speech, but he was not picking up anything this time around.

"Mom, I'm really sorry, but I just don't understand what you're saying."

"Ah leev you." Dylan had heard this one before. It was a phrase he made sure he understood when he was growing up.

"I love you too, mom," he responded. "Is everything OK?"

Without a response, Dylan heard a click and then the dial tone. He stared at the receiver blankly, wondering what that was all about. Usually his mother stammered and talked until Dylan finally got a little of what she was trying to say. This time she just seemed to give up.

While Dylan was processing this he heard a knock on the door.

"It's open," he yelled. He heard the jiggle of the door handle and a push against the door.

"No it's not, man," John said on the other side. "Let me in."

"No, man, it's really unlocked. You just gotta push harder." Again he heard the rattle of the door. "Harder," Dylan yelled, wondering how long he could get John to do this.

"Seriously?!" John said rattling the door even harder. "What am I doing wrong?"

Dylan chuckled to himself before finally unlocking the deadbolt and opening the door for his gullible friend.

"You're a real asshole, you know that, right?" John said.

"Just as God made me, sir."

"So we ready to do this thing?" John said hitting his fist to his palm.

"I guess so, what do we have to lose, right? What the hell are you wearing?"

Dylan looked at his friend, who was wearing a bandana, a green denim army jacket, camouflage pants and snow boots. He had a length of rope wrapped around him, a combat knife strapped to his leg and a strip of black shoe polish under each eye.

"What do you mean, man? I'm ready for battle, you don't know what it's gonna be like down there. We could wind up in a real jam and we gotta be ready for anything."

"You just seem a little overdressed is all. I think all we're gonna do is watch these people. I don't think any of us is ready to go flying into the bowels of Hell dressed like GI Joe's little brother."

"Make jokes all you want, man, but you'll be thanking me when the shit hits the fan."

"You're still drunk from last night aren't you?" Dylan asked.

"Yes I am."

"Well, that's reassuring," Dylan responded.

Chris then walked up, holding a cup of coffee and wearing a backpack.

"What's up fellas? Ready to do this?"

John and Dylan nodded to Chris.

"Cool, let's roll…what the hell are you wearing?"

Chris, Dylan and John crouched down low in the bushes with a pair of binoculars, hoping not to be spotted. They had watched the Line for about a half hour now as two separate groups of travelers had risen out of the Exit. Chris told them he thought each set was smaller and more heavily guarded with Watchers than usual. John's rope and combat knife had yet to be of use.

Dylan had borrowed a set of clothes from Chris, an orange jump suit designed to look like the travelers, just in case the opportunity presented itself to jump into the Line. John, of course was not letting Dylan live it down.

"Now who looks ridiculous?" he gloated. "You stick out like a sore thumb, dude. At least I'm wearing camouflage."

"Do you see anyone else down there wearing camo?" Chris asked.

"Let me check," John said crouching down and attempting to keep the binoculars steady enough so he could see clearly. His hands shook clearly showing signs of alcohol withdrawals after another typically wild night.

Dylan, who had become all too familiar with John's exploits, knew exactly that John's hands couldn't sit still.

"Did shit get weird last night, John?" Dylan asked. "Anything you want to share about last night, or should I just read about it on your blog?"

"I don't post things about my love life on my blog. It's dedicated solely to the art of sneaking," he said.

"Sneaking?" Chris asked

"I'll send you a link," Dylan said.

"I wasn't even that drunk, really," John said. "Well, not at first. Janelle came over and… I'd really rather not talk about it. Jesus, this is impossible, did either of you guys bring a tripod?"

Chris and Dylan looked at each other and shrugged, suggesting that neither had thought to bring any sort of device to control John's shaking hands.

"Well shit then," John said. "I can't do this, I'm gonna go over there and be the lookout again." John handed the binoculars to Chris, lit up a Camel light and leaned against a nearby tree. It was good to know their lookout was so on top of things.

"So what do you think?" Dylan asked Chris. "Do you think I could make it in there?"

"I just don't think that's a good idea today. Seems pretty heavy and I'm not sure we should try it on your first time out. Besides, you seem like you're in too good of a mood."

"You keep saying that man, and I'm telling you, I'm as miserable as they get. I think I'll be fine."

"Let's just sit tight for a bit."

"You ever wonder what they're doing?" Dylan asked Chris.

"All of the time." Chris responded.

"Any conclusions?"

"Not really," Chris said. "Like I said, I've never made it down there, so I have little to go off of. I always think about what else could possibly exist if the Line really does lead to Hell."

"What do you mean?" Dylan asked.

"You ever read *Lord of the Flies*?" Chris asked.

"I guess so, maybe in school. It's been awhile."

"Do you know that part where the fat kid, Piggy, talks about the monster on the island being real?"

"Totally," Dylan said, not having any idea what he was talking about. He wasn't actually sure he had ever read the book at all.

"There's that part where they're convinced there is a monster on the island, and they all start losing their minds. Piggy says that if the beast is real, then what does that mean for the rest of the normal world: houses, schools, trees. It just wouldn't make sense in the natural world. I'm paraphrasing of course."

"Of course," Dylan said still very confused.

"Well this doesn't make sense with the rest of our natural, boring-ass world," Chris said motioning to the Line. "If this exists, why is everything else still the same? Why is this so mundane, when it's supposed to be so magical. If this is Hell then where is Heaven? Where is God, how come he hasn't shown up yet?"

While Dylan was still trying to process what Chris was getting at, John wandered over." You shall not pass!" he bellowed.

"What?" Dylan asked looking very confused.

"Gandalf the Gray, dude. I heard you guys talking about *Lord of the Rings*. I love those movies. I've never been able to sit through one all the way to the end though."

Chris smiled slightly, realizing further literary comparisons would be wasted on this audience. "You believe in God, John?" he asked. John paused for a second.

"You know," he began. "I never really thought about it."

"Never really thought about it?" Dylan said to him. "You've never once wondered about the existence of God?"

"No, not really. I mean, if I was to give you an answer now, I'd say sure, why not?"

Dylan looked over at Chris and shook his head. "You see what I have to put up with all of the time?"

"You're a saint," Chris said. Taking the binoculars and looking down from the hill onto the Line, Chris noticed something strange. "Well this is weird," he said aloud.

"What is?" Dylan asked.

"Someone's making a break for it," the three men looked down and saw that one of the Inhabitants was sprinting away from the Line in an attempt to escape. Three guards were giving chase. The rest of the line was commanded to stop.

"This may sound crazy, but I think now's your chance. That guy is pulling everyone's attention away. It'll be a couple minutes before they're back and marching."

"Now?"

"Now! Go!"

With the subtle prompting, Dylan took off down the hill, following a cover of trees that Chris instructed he hide behind. He raced to the bottom of the hill and stopped short when he was within a few feet of a pair of dead-eyed Travelers and hid motionless behind a leafy pine tree. He heard shouting from a few yards ahead getting closer. It seemed that the guards had already caught the escapee and were heading back in his direction.

With no armed Watchers in sight, Dylan took a deep breath and stepped in between two Travelers towards the back of the line. Just then, the guards came back, dragging the man who had tried to run. "Put this asshole between Charles and Drake," one of the guards said as he shoved him between two Watchers about twenty feet in front of Dylan. "If he tries that shit again, beat him until his eyes pop out of his head. No more surface passes for you, buddy boy," the guard said shoving him back in line. "Let's move!" he yelled, and one by one, everyone resumed their slow, dead march.

Dylan had done it. He had accomplished something for the first time in his life. He was so happy.

From on top of the hill, Chris watched him from the binoculars. "Did he make it?" John asked from behind him.

"He's in," Chris said turning. "But he's not gonna last long."

"Why? What's wrong?"

"He's smiling," Chris responded. "Pretty soon we'll have to go look for him."

Dylan marched along happy as a school girl for several moments. He couldn't believe this was happening. He was ecstatic about the possibility of what he was about to see. "Why was this so easy?" he thought. "Why had no one done this before?" It was then he realized he was getting very drowsy. His feet felt heavy and he could no longer focus on the Traveler in front of him. His eyes began to close. A few more steps and he could not fight it any longer. Dylan's vision blurred, his eyes shut tight and everything went black.

Chapter 14

"He told me he heard a voice that made him do it," Lawrence Thompson, the Essex County Correctional Facility psychologist, was telling Warden Alan Dormeus about David Estern.

"Classic schizo, huh?" The warden asked him.

"I'm not sure," Thompson continued. "He said it wasn't the Devil directly, but the voice that he talks to knows the Devil, says he works with him. Something about a dragon. He clearly has some psychological issues. We can't, in good conscience, execute him."

"Then why didn't he say that in any of the proceedings? Why did he only tell you," the warden asked.

"I'm not sure, but we need more time, we can't kill this man."

The warden and Lawrence Thompson rarely saw eye to eye on anything. The warden was constantly accusing Lawrence of being too soft, a hippie. They had fought tooth and nail over the institution of the PHP project, but the warden eventually acquiesced, knowing that at the end of the day it saved them money, and that was his primary concern. He strongly believed in the death penalty and did not appreciate Lawrence's intrusion into the David Estern case. It had taken two years of cutting through red tape to send him to the death chamber. And while this was exceptionally quick in the grand scheme of things, the warden didn't want the execution to be delayed any further.

"Sounds nuttier than a shit-house rat to me," the warden said. "I can't have this guy living out the rest of his days in a comfy nut house in Binghampton. I need to juice this one."

"It's my job to assess each situation fairly and accurately. If I think he's faking it to save himself then I will tell you, but, if I believe this man truly believes he hears voices, then I need to say that as well."

"Well, do what you gotta do, I guess. Let me know what you find out," the warden said. "Give 'em hell, buddy."

Lawrence Thompson rose from his chair, shook the warden's hand and said, "Let's hope it doesn't come to that."

Lawrence Thompson walked down the light blue carpet that stretched from end to end over the otherwise dull, gray concrete that covered death row. The color was picked out by the PHP project to ease inmate's transition to the "other side." It was supposed to represent hope, tranquility and Heaven. Most people called it the Smurf Dick.

He was on his way to speak with David Estern, to get further information about this alleged voice he had heard. His shoes hit heavy on the hard floor and rattled the crucifix hung above the door; Jesus Christ's plaster eyes watched the scene with casual interest.

He reached a security door at the end of the hallway and hit a small red intercom button to let the volunteer on duty know that he was there.

"Who is it?" said the sweet southern accent through the box.

"It's Lawrence" he said. "Who's that?"

"Oh, hey Lawrence, it's Deborah," replied Deborah Collins, the church organist. "I'm the only one here. There was a guard down here this morning, but I haven't seen him in hours."

"Think you could let me in?"

"I think so. Which button is it again?"

"Um, ya know, I'm not sure. I'm pretty sure it says door 6, but it might be 7."

There was a pause on the other end as Deborah fumbled with a series of buttons. Then, Lawrence heard a whir or gears and the door in front of him slid open.

"Did that do it?" Deborah asked, unaware that Lawrence was already through the door and on his way towards her. "Hello?" Lawrence walked into the small hallway just before the death row cells and found Deborah still trying to talk to him through the intercom.

"Hello? Lawrence? You there, sweetheart?"

"Right here, Deborah," he said from behind her.

"Oh Lord!" Deborah said, turning with her hand on her heart. "You startled me!"

"Sorry about that. Obviously wasn't my intention. How's he doing today?

"Who, the murderer? Fine, I guess. Haven't really heard a peep out of him since I been here. I tell you what, though. I ain't been trying to talk to him much. That man gives me the creeps."

"We have to help these people, Deborah, no matter what they might have done. Why don't you head home for the night? It's getting late. I'll tell the guard on duty, if I see him."

"I think I might just do that. Gotta get home and watch my stories anyway. Good night Lawrence. God bless you."

"Thank you," he responded.

Although Lawrence appreciated the extra help the PHP project afforded him, he really couldn't stand the religious hue that it had recently taken on. Why people couldn't just be good on their own without having to rely on the help of Jesus was always confusing to him. He waited until Deborah had cleared the security door before walking down the narrow corridor and up to David Estern's cell.

When he arrived, he peered through the glass window leading in and saw David laying on his bunk facing away from the door, obscuring his face. He opened the cell door's receiving window with a key, and, as he pushed it open, Estern spoke to him without turning around. "Evening Lawrence."

"Hello, David. How'd you know it was me?"

"Just intuition, I guess. Besides, I don't get a lot of guests down here, just those religious nuts you have trying to save my soul."

"They're just trying to do their part. Trying to make your final days a little easier."

"How many of those days do you think I have left?"

"Well that depends, David. It all depends on whether I think you're telling the truth or not about the voices."

"Voice," David corrected. "Just one voice. I know what I heard. I'm not crazy, at least I wasn't. Who knows anymore?"

"Well David, if you truly believe that the voice you heard is really there, then I can recommend that you are not mentally fit to be executed, and you will be taken off death row and transferred to a state mental facility. It's not exactly Club Med, but it will give you a chance to get better."

"Well, that's just not gonna work. That's not part of the plan," David said.

"What plan would that be?"

David finally turned towards Lawrence, got off his bunk and walked over to the cell door. "I have a feeling that if you keep interfering you'll hear all about it very soon."

Chapter 15

Lauren was sitting in her room, concerned about the day's events. She'd hoped action wasn't taken regarding the gift-shop employee and his contact with her.

Vast hallways cut through the caverns in Hell, displaying nauseatingly bright track lighting that never turned off but would occasionally flicker in brightness. The living quarters were set up like jail cells, jammed on top of each other for hundreds of miles. It was the suburbs of a nonexistent city stretching on infinitely. She lay on her bunk and thought about how she had gotten there in the first place; it was Kevin's fault. Things were great when they started. She even thought they were actually in love, and maybe they were. She remembered things going down hill really quickly. She never knew how ugly they could get. If she could take back that one night, she would. One night defined the rest of her life and was making her after-life pretty intolerable. If only she hadn't...

"Hey, gorgeous," said Artie, standing at Lauren's open door and completely interrupting her train of thought.

"This is my room Artie. You can't just walk into my room and bother me, it's rude."

"The door was open," he said. "I thought you were waiting for me."

"I thought I made myself pretty clear last time that that was not going to happen. Do I need to get something sharp to further drive the point home?"

"Whoa, take it easy. I come in peace," Artie said throwing his hands up in mock surrender. "I just thought you'd like to know what I heard about the surface passes, considering your little boyfriend and all."

"What about them?" Lauren said angrily but sitting up with genuine concern.

"Just that they're not gonna be so easy to get anymore. They're putting a cap on them and only giving them out to those with exemplary records, i.e., people who don't consort with surface dwellers every chance they get, i.e., you."

"What are you getting at, Artie?"

"All I have to do is tell the counselor that you have repeatedly talked to the gift-shop boy and it's bye bye surface and bye bye boyfriend."

"You'd be lying then," she said.

"We all know what we're supposed to do when someone from the surface talks to us. Smiling and winking is not exactly protocol," Artie said, crossing his arms in a smug fashion. "They're looking for any excuse to deny people access to the surface. Don't make me give them one."

"What do you want?" Lauren asked.

"You know what I want," said Artie attempting to look seductive. "I want what I've always wanted." Artie then reached out his hands and tried to touch Lauren around the waist.

"Don't you fucking touch me," Lauren angrily responded, slapping Artie's hands away and delivering a sharp shove to his chest. "I can do the same thing you know. I can make up a lie about you and make sure you never see the surface again. Jay and I are pretty good friends these days."

"That may be," Artie began, "but I've become quite bored with the surface and, unlike you, I don't have some impossible dream about escaping. I'm perfectly content here. If I knew that you'd be sticking around as well, I could be happy for a while." Artie again tried to make an advance at Lauren, who responded with a quick kick to Artie's balls, doubling him over and sending him crashing to the floor.

"Creep!" Lauren yelled as she stepped over him, out the door and directly towards the line to counselor Stevenson's office. She was going to get to the bottom of this.

After several hours of waiting in line, Lauren had finally reached the counselor's office. She simply could not bear the thought of never seeing the surface again. She was worried that her brief encounters with the gift-shop employee had ruffled some feathers and that it would be enough to keep her out of the Line forever. She just couldn't handle that. She would go crazy. She knew the counselor liked her, though, so she would have to exploit it. She put on her biggest smile and was ready to flirt her way to another surface pass. She would do whatever it took.

"Next!" shouted the guard at the front of the counselor's office, as another Inhabitant walked out of the room. Lauren passed by the muscle-bound guard and into the office. The counselor, as usual, looked frazzled and overworked. She smiled a big toothy grin at him, which quickly went away when she saw who else was in the room with him.

Standing in the shadows behind the counselor was Neville Black. Lauren had seen him wander through Hell's hallways before, but had never spoken to him. She realized this was the closest she had ever been to him. He was much paler up close.

"Ms. Adams," the counselor said without making eye contact. "Please have a seat."

"Thanks, Jay!" Lauren began. "It's really good to see you! How are you?"

The counselor shifted uncomfortably in his seat and slightly glanced over his shoulder at Neville Black who looked appalled. "Please, Ms. Adams," the counselor said nervously. "You must address me as counselor Stevenson, just like everybody else."

"But I thought..."

"Please adhere to the rules Ms. Adams," Neville interrupted her. Lauren turned to face Jay, who still refused to make eye contact with her. It was clear that Mr. Black's presence was forcing the counselor to change his tone with her. Lauren knew this couldn't be a good sign and probably had something to do with what Artie had told her earlier in the day. Mr. Black was here to police the meetings and make sure the counselor followed the new set of rules. Lauren knew this was not a good thing.

"What can we do for you, Ms. Adams?" The counselor asked.

Caught off guard, Lauren had forgotten why she was there. "Um, I'd like a surface pass, please.

Counselor Stevenson, looking embarrassed, rose from his chair to retrieve Lauren's personal file from a cabinet behind his desk.

"There have been some changes in the policy, Ms. Adams," Mr. Black said, while Jay rifled through the massive filing cabinet.

"Like what?" Lauren asked.

"Only Inhabitants with exemplary records will be issued surface passes from here on out. Even the slightest blemish could result in termination of the program for that Inhabitant permanently."

Upon retrieving Lauren's file, the counselor returned to his desk and sat back in his chair with a heavy sigh. Lauren swallowed hard as he surveyed the notes he had written on the top page of her file. He did this for several minutes and then finally spoke. "Ms. Adams. I regret to inform you that your request for a surface pass has been denied."

"What?" Lauren shouted. "What did I do?"

"It has been reported by another Inhabitant that you were seen consorting with a surface dweller on more than one occasion, and, in light of recent restrictions, we feel this is grounds to suspend your privilege."

"What Inhabitant?" Lauren demanded. "Who, Artie? You're gonna listen to that guy? Come on, Jay. That guy has some sick obsession with me. He's doing this whole thing..."

"Please, Ms. Adams!" Jay shouted. "It's counselor Stevenson to you!"

Lauren stopped and put her head down. Mr. Black, looking pleased with the situation, arose from the side table he was leaning on and stood behind the counselor, putting his hands on his shoulders.

"Please, Ms. Adams. Listen to your counselor. He has your best interest in mind. Now if you'll excuse me," he said walking towards the door of the counselor's office, "I have other matters to attend to. Good day." Mr. Black then closed the door behind him and left the room in awkward silence.

Lauren did not lift her head to look at the counselor when she finally spoke. "How could you do this to me?" she whispered solemnly.

"It's not me Lauren, it's them," he responded.

"Don't call me Lauren," she said sharply back.

A few more moments of awkward silence followed before the counselor opened the drawer to his desk and retrieved a pad of paper that he began writing on. "What are you doing?" she asked.

"This could be your last one for awhile, Ms. Adams, so make the most of it," he said as he handed her a surface pass he had just filled out.

"Thank you, Jay," Lauren politely responded.

"You're welcome. I'm sorry it had to come to this."

"Like you said, it's not you. It's them." Lauren leapt at Jay and gave him a huge hug, almost knocking over his desk. Acts of kindness like this were not common in Hell.

She needed to get out of the office before he changed his mind and she released her grip on him and turned to leave.

As she reached towards the door handle, Jay spoke to her.

"Lauren," he said as she turned back towards him, "please don't make me regret this."

"I can't promise that, Jay. Sorry," she said and hurried out of the door.

Chapter 16

Dylan heard screams all around him and smelled burning. The heat that he felt was overwhelming, pulsing through his body and tingling the tips of his bones.

He looked around the cavernous room and saw corpses everywhere. Bodies, stripped of their flesh, laying limp and rotting in piles all around him, dead but still moving. The lumps of flesh lay writhing and squirming, reaching skeletal hands towards Dylan and attempting to grab him and pull him closer. The shrieks were impenetrable, thousands of them all piercing Dylan's ears, demanding help, pleading for solace that no one could offer.

From behind the largest pile of mangled corpses, Dylan saw movement from within. One of them was rising and coming for him. Dylan took a step back and was about to run when from behind the pile of flesh stepped Easy Money - wearing a tuxedo and picking his orange afro with a pearl white pick. "S'up, patnah?" he said.

"Hey, what the fuck are you doing here?" Dylan said.

"I'd ask you the same question, bitch. What the fuck you think you're doing messing around like this? Always running from something, ain't ya?"

"I'm not running from anything," Dylan said. "I'm walking towards something. At least I was walking. How did I get here?"

"Oh you ain't nowhere. You're just dreaming. Why the hell you think I look so damn good?"

"But I made it. I'm here... aren't I?"

"Man, hell no, you failed again. Damn it, Dylan, when you gonna learn to just be happy with where you're at?"

"I am. Well, I'm not, but I think I will be, maybe"

"Damn shame, my brother. Remember what I say, always keep that head up, especially now. Which reminds me, watch out," Easy Money said.

"For what?" Dylan asked.

The sudden jolt caused Dylan to crash ass first to the ground. He awoke from his dream and found himself lying on a moss covered rock in the middle of the woods. His head was pounding, and he felt a fresh trickle of blood run down his face. The tree he had just run into swayed slightly before him. He didn't think he had ever walked in his sleep, but this is clearly what had happened. He didn't even remember going to bed. He wondered if he was drunk and he felt like he was. He slowly sat up and surveyed his surroundings.

Dylan saw nothing but the blurred black lines of tree-hugging pine needles and heard nothing but traffic on a far-off highway. His body hurt. He reached down and picked out a few pine needles from his clothing. How the Hell did he end up here?

He heard a rustle coming from the deep brush next to him. Dylan wondered if he should turn and run the other direction. He didn't know how he would eventually die, but wandering off into the woods and getting mauled by a pack of raccoons was the last way he wanted to go out. The rustling grew louder, and Dylan knew something big was coming towards him. He took a step backwards and looked frantically for something to defend himself with. He settled on a medium sized rock, and, as his animal assailant got nearer, he hurled it as hard as he could at the approaching beast.

"Ow, fuck!" The bush said as John emerged holding his head with Chris right behind him.

"See why I wanted you to go first?" Chris said to John.

"Guys!" Dylan said excitedly, "What the fuck?! Where am I?"

"You're a few miles from highway 90, I think Brinton is that way," Chris said turning around a few times."

"Did I make it? I mean, what happened with the Line? Who, I mean, where?...Christ, my head hurts," Dylan finally relaxed, putting his hand upon his fresh tree wound."

"Yeah, that makes two of us," John said looking menacingly at Dylan.

"Sorry, man. I thought you were a bear or something."

"That's the thanks I get for coming to rescue you," John said.

"Rescue me? I still don't understand what happened. Chris, what went wrong?"

"The Line rejected you man," Chris said. "Your mind wasn't in the right place. I told you, it knows."

"Well we gotta fix that then. I was so close."

"You weren't that close man," Chris said. "I'm pretty sure the exit is still like a mile away from here."

"I blacked out," Dylan said. "How long was I walking like that?"

"No way to tell," Chris said. "We watched you for awhile and then eventually you just veered off the course. You were tough to keep up with. I'm glad we found you.

"Well, we gotta try again, right?

"If you want to, but first we gotta talk about some things," Chris said.

"Yeah, like what?" Dylan asked.

"Why your life sucks so bad."

"I'm just not sure that's gonna do it for me," Dylan said as John fiddled with the DVD player.

"What dude?" John responded. "This is one of the saddest movies of all time. I cry every time I see it. If this doesn't make you sad, nothing will."

The men had returned to Chris' apartment with a plan to delve into Dylan's personal life in an attempt to unearth some personal demons, leaving Dylan sad, miserable and Line ready. Dylan, like always refused to open up. Luckilly, John had a different plan.

"I'm just not sure I'll be able to really get into this," Dylan responded, picking up the DVD case to *My Girl*.

"This is guaranteed to make you cry," John said in protest. "Those fucking bees sure do a number on little Macaulay."

"Well, you just gave away what seems to be a pretty vital plot point so what's the point of watching it now?" Dylan asked.

"Oh, yeah, good point. Well, you don't know how the bees get him. Forget I said anything. There are no bees."

Dylan looked over at Chris for some validation that it was not just him who thought the things John said were completely idiotic, but Chris, knowing that Dylan's eyes were on him, just shook his head in confusion as he read the synopsis on the back of the DVD case to *Untamed Heart*, another one of John's selections.

"Is this gonna work, Chris?" Dylan finally asked. "Or are we completely off track?"

"Depends," he responded. "I mean, I don't think watching the *Home Alone* kid get killed by bees will make you sad enough to trick the Line into thinking you're as hopeless as the rest of them. But maybe something will resonate with you on another level. Maybe one of these scenes will remind you of something that will."

"I guess at this point, I'll try anything," Dylan said.

"Outside of general curiosity, why do you want to get into Hell so badly?" Chris finally asked. "Why is this so important?"

"No reason really," Dylan said. "Like you said, just curiosity. I want to see what it's like. Also, maybe it will get me somewhere or something, like an award or money or..."

"Or a girl," John said, cutting Dylan off.

"It has nothing to do with her," Dylan said sharply to John.

"Who is her?" Chris asked.

"Dylan has a crush on one of them. On one of the Hell babes. He tries to talk to her all of the time."

"You've talked to one of the Walkers?" Chris asked sitting up in his chair.

"Oh, he hasn't talked to her," John said. "That would require someone saying words back or even acknowledging the other's presence. She totally ignores him."

"Well, I wouldn't get too offended, Dylan," Chris said. "I think people have been trying to get those people to talk for decades and have never gotten a word. I'm not even sure they can actually, or maybe they're forbidden to. Maybe if we finally get you down there you can find out for sure."

"Well, I'm not gonna hold my breath for that," Dylan said. "I haven't ever been successful at anything. I'm sure this won't be any different. Once a loser, always a loser." Dylan scratched his head and let out a heavy sigh.

"I think we're on the right track here, guys. John, cue the bees," Chris said.

Dylan awoke to a blue screen on John's television. He looked around and noticed that John and Chris had both fallen asleep as well. So much for John's plan. Dylan had barely made it past the opening credits before he passed out. He tried to think about the initial feeling of hopelessness that Chris had pointed out he was feeling earlier. As he thought about it, it wasn't enough. He had always taken his station in life with a grain of salt and a sense of humor. Sure, it wasn't great, but if he really thought about what he did for a living it was pretty comical.

He smiled to himself and flipped the button on the remote to take the TV off DVD mode so he could watch cable while the others slept. He flipped through the channels quickly, not really looking for anything specifically, but hoping he could find something with nudity. As the various volumes swelled with each channel, John and Chris began to open their eyes and awake from their respective naps.

"Morning, sleepy heads," Dylan said in a high pitched voice.

"Oh man, I totally passed out," John said. "I guess I usually sleep a lot after I cry that much."

"It was an emotional moment for us all," Dylan said.

"What are you still doing here? Shouldn't you be hopelessly wandering around the caverns of Hell at this point?"

"I guess watching, knowing that Macaulay is still alive and kicking in real life, made it so no tears were shed," Dylan said and continued to flip through the channels before finally giving up hope of finding anything decent on and settling on an episode of *The Apprentice* that he had already seen before.

"Not me," Chris said sitting up. "I thought it was riveting. Great plan, John. Pure brilliance."

"Shut up," John said.

As the three of them watched Donald Trump berate a room full of entrepreneurial hopefuls, John pointed towards the screen, "That girl kinda looks like Monica."

"A little bit," Dylan responded knowing exactly which girl he was talking about. Directly in front of Trump's desk was a blonde woman with piercing eyes and a fiery smile reminiscent of Dylan's ex-girlfriend.

"Who is Monica?" Chris asked.

"A girl I used to date," Dylan said.

"She was THE girl that Dylan used to date," John explained. "That girl shattered him, broke him in two."

"Shut the fuck up John," Dylan said.

"What's going on here?" Chris asked.

"Dylan doesn't like to talk about Monica," John said. "It didn't end well. She cheated on him."

Chris saw this as an opportunity to delve into the situation and see how far he could push Dylan on the subject. He wanted to see if he could change his mood.

"Tell me about her, man," Chris said. "What exactly happened?"

"There's not a lot to tell, really…" Dylan said before pausing and trying to find the words. "She just, got tired of me. I can't say I blame her, really. Most people do at some point."

Without trying to distract from the situation, Chris slowly rose and walked over to Dylan.

"Hold that thought Dylan," he said putting his hand on Dylan's shoulder. "I think you're ready."

Chapter 17

Lauren didn't know what to do. This could be her last visit to the surface, and that was something she couldn't handle. She had seen how people started to act after they had been in Hell too long. They started to lose themselves. Their spirits broke. It's tough to retain any sort of normalcy in Hell, but Lauren had always thought she had done a pretty good job of it. If she never got to see the light of day again, she knew she'd go crazy.

When she was alive, she had read *Man's Search for Meaning* by Victor Frankl for a freshman Psychology class at Rutgers. The book tells of Frankl's experience while at Auschwitz and how he had to condition his mind not to accept the reality that was around him. Lauren had tried to use this philosophy while she was in Hell. But she wasn't sure how much longer she could maintain a positive mental attitude, especially with the thought that she may never see daylight again.

She was angry. If it wasn't for that fucking gift-shop employee, none of this would have happened. She had vowed, after her last relationship ended so violently, she would never involve herself with a man ever again. She was starting to remember why once again.

As her thoughts raced, she started to think of a plan. It was a solution she had thought of before on Earth and, while it was never successful, if tweaked a bit, could help her current situation. She dug under her mattress and retrieved a small, sharpened stone she had kept there for protection from people like Artie. She ran her finger over the jagged edge. It was still sharp.

She knew it was going to hurt but she was desperate. She took a deep breath and began to cut into her skin.

She had lost a lot of blood and was woozy. The stone was not as sharp as it once was, and it took some effort to carve up certain parts of her message. She felt a trickle of blood ooze down her neck and quickly wiped it away with her hand. No one could see it until the time was right. This was the first part of her plan, but she didn't exactly know how the rest would shape up. She was waiting in line, for her chance to ascend to the surface.

"Head up! Remain upright! Do not break stride, and please mind the Inhabitant in front of you! If you break any of these rules, a Watcher will escort you from the Line and your surface pass will be revoked. Please keep moving."

The rhetoric at this point mostly fell on deaf ears, as most of the Inhabitants marched along zombie-like, having been through the process before. To Lauren, the words were deafening, and she hoped it wasn't the last time she heard them.

A commotion ran through the guards as they looked off into the distance and began whispering to one another.

"All Inhabitants, please stand aside!" A guard shouted. "Our Lord and Leader approaches! Fall to your knees and embrace the Dark Lord!"

Daman and Neville Black were approaching. The faint sounds of a guitar solo got louder. The Inhabitants groaned and begrudgingly got to their knees and bowed their heads. Lauren, worried that if Neville saw her and recognized her from Jay's office, ducked her head down and tucked her chin against her chest. She didn't dare look up.

"I have arrived! You may be seated."

"Um, sorry my Lord," a guard said. "Out of respect for your arrival, I actually instructed them to kneel. I thought it was appropriate for the situation."

"I see," Daman said slightly embarrassed, as he realized he should have been more observant. "Then you shall remain kneeling, but heed my words with care as I will only utter them once." After saying this, it was clear Daman may have forgotten what he came to talk about as he stood there wagging his finger for several moments before he finally whispered to Mr. Black, "What are dey to be heeding again?""

"About the new order, sir. About how things are going to be different."

"Ah, yes," he said quietly. "De new order." Daman then made a quick turn back towards the Line, spreading his cloak wide in the process. "There is to be a new order sweeping over de underworld! We have been too soft. Now we will be harder than ever. We will be so very rock hard!"

A few of the Inhabitants in the Line snickered. Daman did not understand what was funny. "Silence!"" he shouted and then turned and whispered to Mr. Black again. "Why are dey laughing? What have I said?"

"Oh, it's nothing, sir," Mr. Black said "I think they're just laughing out of fear."

"Ah, yes. I am very fearful," he said. He again turned towards the Line. "From now on, we will treat you as you deserve to be treated. We will torture more, we will feed less and we will turn up the lights even brighter. Your heads will ache with pain muahahahahahahaha..." As Daman let out his final menacing laugh, he began to cough violently. "Water!" cough, cough. "please," cough, "Mr. Black," cough, "Water."

Mr. Black looked panicked for a second before cupping his hands together, dipping them under a nearby water cooler and placing them under Daman's mouth, allowing him to sip gingerly from them, like he was feeding a giant kitten. Even Lauren, who was terrified of being recognized, held her head up for a few moments and watched the spectacle that was taking place.

After the water was gone and Daman stopped drinking, he spoke again. "No longer will we tolerate de insubordination. No longer will we allow de misgivings. We will remain hard and give it to you hard like you deserve."

This again caused the Line to start laughing.

"Yes, dat is right. De fear makes you laugh. You will not be laughing when we are tru with you. You will suffer!"

The Line suddenly stopped laughing. Although he could be comical at times, it was clear Daman was intent on making their already miserable existence far worse.

"Dat is all," Daman spoke again. "Enjoy de Earth. It may be de last time you ever see it."

Chapter 18

Dylan had been, for the most part, silent as he gazed listlessly out of the window of Chris's car. He watched the bleak scenery of Brinton and thought about Monica. He hated being reminded of her. Despite the subject being touchy, John and Chris, hoping to keep Dylan on the verge of tears, were picking away at the core of him.

"I mean, if I really think about it, I never really loved her," Dylan said at one point. "I just liked the security she gave me. I liked coming home and having someone there."
"Yeah, but I can't imagine the thought of the woman I loved being with someone else," Chris said. "What if you never fall in love again? Man, that would be just tragic."
Dylan turned his face to the car window and fought back a few welling tears. Chris really knew what he was doing. While they drove, Chris continued to throw barbs about Monica to Dylan, trying to keep him in his current state, while John had a different strategy.
In the last half hour, John had mentioned to Dylan a myriad of topics he considered tragic and equally tear-jerking. John casually brought up such topics as the plight of the people of Somalia, Pearl Harbor, animal testing and Shun Fujimoto, who won a gold medal at the 1976 Olympic Games despite having a broken foot.
"You think Shun Fujimoto would have let go of the woman she loved?! Hell no! You'll never be as brave as fucking Shun Fujimoto, Dylan!"
They drove to what Chris considered a prime spot for watching. It was close to where they had previously been, where Dylan had

wandered off into the Pine Barrens. Because of the last time, they had a rough understanding of how to get back to town in case Dylan wandered off again. They guessed from where they were that the entrance to Hell was only a few miles away. They set up their binoculars and waited for the outpouring of Walkers to begin. Dylan did not watch the Line with the others, but instead chose to sit with his back against a tree, facing away from the Line and staring off into the distance, lost in state of deep philosophical sadness. "Hey John," he finally said.

"Yeah, buddy?" he answered.

"You never knew your mom, did you?" Dylan asked him.

"Yeah, I did, I mean, when I was little. She died when I was three, I don't really remember her."

"I feel like I'm not there for mine, and she's the only parent I have left," Dylan said.

"My dad did a great job raising me," John said. "Who knows what I would've been like if he hadn't been around. I might have some serious problems."

"I'm not sure if I love my mom," Dylan said.

"Sure you do, man. Come on, that's crazy. Your mom is great."

"Ok, you're right, I do, but I don't know if she really loves me."

"What are you talking about?"

"You know what I'm talking about," Dylan said. "She has no way of telling me anything, she's practically a vegetable. There's no way for her to tell me what's going on inside her head. I think sometimes she tells me she loves me, but she could just as easily be telling me about what she had for lunch that day. There's no way for her to tell me anything or to teach me anything."

"Teach you things?" John asked.

"You know those people who are always saying 'My dad taught me the value of a dollar' or 'my mom told me always judge a man by the type of shoes he wears.' My mom never had a way to teach me about life, and my dad died too early to ever say anything. They never had a chance to tell me what I am supposed to be doing with my life."

"Always learn the janitor's name," Chris said.

"Huh?" said Dylan.

"Always learn the janitor's name. That was my dad's big advice to me. He said that if I treated the lesser people at any job I had with respect, that people would take notice and think it showed character. He also said that janitors had all the keys and could open any door in the building for you."

"That's actually pretty smart," Dylan said. "Where's he now?"

"Dead – last year."

"Jesus, man, I'm sorry. How?" Dylan asked.

"You remember that earthquake that hit the East Coast last year in August?"

"Yeah, that was nuts!" John interjected. "Remember, Dylan, we were at the mall and we thought it was a truck driving through?"

"Wait, your dad died in that?" Dylan asked. "I thought it just damaged a few buildings. It seemed pretty tame. There were casualties?"

"None that were reported," Chris said. "They eventually deemed that it wasn't a direct result of the quake, so it didn't count."

"So how did he die?" Dylan asked.

"In the house that I grew up in, my parents had this huge brass scale. It must've weighed 80 pounds. We had it forever, ever since I was a kid. When I was real young, I was fascinated with it and would always go over and try to play with it. Obviously this was not something a toddler should be playing with, so my mom kept moving it up higher and higher on the shelf the bigger I got. Eventually, I stopped caring and we just sorta forgot about it.

When the quake hit, as small as it was, the shelves started rattling in my parent's house. My dad was sitting below it, working at the computer or something, and it rattled loose, fell down off the highest shelf and hit him right on the head. He died of blunt force trauma right there on the spot."

"Man, that's horrible," Dylan said. "No chance for anyone. Fuck this place." He walked over to an oak, sat down underneath it and put his head in hands.

John didn't like seeing his friend like this. Although he knew he was not the smartest person in the world, he knew that he could always cheer Dylan up. It was one of the few things he was good at. Seeing his friend was in need of a good pep talk, he started walking over to him to console him.

"Dylan," he began. "There's some things you need to know." he then stopped as he heard Chris let out a short cough to get his attention. When he glanced over, he saw that Chris was shaking his head, hoping to remind John that they needed to keep Dylan in this state if they wanted to pull this off. John nodded his head and looked back over at Dylan, who was waiting to hear what his life-long friend was about to tell him.

"What is it man?" Dylan asked in anticipation.

"Dylan, shut the fuck up. You've been whining all day and it's getting fucking old." John, knowing that he had done the correct thing gave a smile a thumbs up over to Chris who nodded his head in assurance that indeed he had passed the test.

Chris turned back around and looked again through his binoculars in the direction of the Line. For a few moments, it was inactive and then the first Inhabitant appeared through a break in the trees.

"Here we go," Chris said.

"Who we got today?" asked John.

"More of the same, it looks like," responded Chris. "They seem

pretty sparse today, looks like we have another short Line. I
wonder what that means."

"Who else is there?" Dylan asked.

"I don't know what she looks like," Chris responded.

"I didn't mean her. I was just wondering if you recognized anyone
else."

"Sure," Chris said.

Dylan tapped him on the shoulder. "May I?" he asked, extending
his hand..

"Yeah," Chris said reluctantly. "Just don't get too excited. Think
about your crappy job and your whore of an ex-girlfriend if you
need to."

Dylan let out a long sigh and took the binoculars from Chris.
"We really should've invested in another pair," John said. "I mean
how much can they really cost?" John had a way of pointing out
the obvious that sometimes eluded people of average to above-
average intelligence.

Dylan looked through the binoculars towards the rock crevice as
new Walkers emerged every few seconds. He had a feeling he
would see the girl he had been waiting for. He tried not to get his
hopes up about it and actually thought it might be better if he
didn't see her. If she didn't show up, that would actually make him
very depressed and most likely help him secure his spot in the
Line. Just then though, she appeared.

"There she is," he said raising his voice. "Chris, she's here."

Chris hustled over to Dylan and grabbed the binoculars from him.
"Where? Which one?"

"The one in the orange jumpsuit," Dylan said.

"You think now's the time to be cracking jokes," Chris asked
Dylan. "How badly do you want to do this?"

"She's like 10 or 12 from the front. The pretty one with blonde hair."

Chris moved the binoculars around until he had zeroed in on the target and finally focused in on Lauren Adams. "She's surrounded, man," Chris said.

"What do you mean?" Dylan asked.

"Surrounded, by Watchers. There are two or three in front of her and another three a few people back. They're watching your girl pretty closely. We may have missed our window."

"Well, what do we do?" Dylan asked exasperated.

"We wait 'til next time."

"Next time? No! Fuck that! I'm going now!"

Before Chris or John had a chance to say anything, Dylan stood up and began to run down the hill. Dylan was not sure himself he knew what he was doing, but he continued to sprint towards Lauren Adams.

"Dylan, wait!" Chris shouted.

He did not look back to hear his friends' shouts and continued running. Chris dropped the binoculars and ran after him. John, not knowing exactly what to do, picked up the binoculars and zoomed in on the frantic chase. No matter what happened, at least he finally got to hold them.

From the top of the hill to her left, Lauren swore she heard shouting. She wanted to look, but was unsure just how close she was to the Watchers.

Dylan finally reached the crowd of Walkers but didn't know what to do next. He was right next to Lauren but didn't know if he should say something to her or step right in line like last time. He had no plan.

Chris had told him there were Watchers all around her, but what did they really do? Last time he spoke to her, no one had reacted.

Why would they this time? How exactly did this work?

"Dylan! Stop!"

He looked and saw Chris running towards him. What did he know? He had never even walked in the Line the entire journey. He was too afraid. Things like this required bravery. He needed to take a chance. Dylan, with little regard for Chris' warnings, took one final step and slid into line right behind Lauren.

This is exactly what Lauren had hoped for. While she knew there were several Watchers close by, she knew this was her only chance and that she needed to do it quickly. Knowing that Dylan was blocking her back from view, she smoothly reached up and lifted the hair off her neck, revealing the message she had carved hours earlier. Still dripping slightly with blood and scabbing in spots, Lauren lifted her hair to reveal a jaggedly carved "HELP ME."

Dylan looked up and was astonished and disgusted. A sharp pain formed in his stomach. Then, something hit him in the head. "Oh shit!" John yelled from on top of the hill as he saw a Watcher retrieve a wooden club from inside of his orange jumpsuit, walk over to Dylan and hit him over the head with it, dropping him to the ground.

Lauren heard the sound and let her hair fall back into place, hoping no one but Dylan had seen it.

Chris stopped in his tracks and shot his hands over his eyes, not wanting to see any more.

Dylan's fall had caused the Line behind him to stop, as his limp body blocked their path. Two other Watchers then got out of their place in Line and picked up Dylan's body to move it. The Watcher who had whacked Dylan walked over in Chris' direction still brandishing the club. "Sir, is this person affiliated with you!"

Chris nodded his head but said nothing.

"The subject has been forcibly subdued for attempting to infiltrate the Line. Further attempts will be dealt with in a more forceful and deadly manner. Do you understand me?"

Chris nodded his head again.

"Your affiliate will be brought over to your location. Sir, do not move," the Watcher said.

The two guards in the back picked up Dylan under his arms and dragged him over towards Chris.

The Watchers stopped about twenty feet from Chris and dropped Dylan on the ground.

"Again, sir," the lead Watcher said. "Please do not infiltrate the Line again or the consequences will be far more severe."

"Got it," Chris said, swallowing hard.

The three Watchers then put their weapons back in their jumpsuits and took their places back in Line. "Forward!" one of them shouted, and the Line continued.

Chris waited for them to be out of site and then ran over to Dylan to survey the damage. Dylan was bleeding slightly around a large knot that had already formed on his head, a galaxy like bruise was beginning to darken. Chris put his head to Dylan's chest to see if he was alive. He heard the familiar bump of a heart beat and felt his chest expand with a slow breath. He was relieved his friend wasn't dead, but wondered if he'd be left with some sort of brain damage.

"Is he OK?" John shouted as he ran down the hill towards them.

"He's alive. But I wouldn't be surprised if he didn't remember any of this when he wakes up."

John reached them and knelt down. "Man, that guy laid him out, huh? I could hear the sound all the way up there."

"Yeah, that wasn't pretty. Can't say I'm surprised it happened with the way he darted into the Line like that. What was he thinking?"

"I don't know. Girls do crazy things to Dylan. Maybe this will make him realize they're not worth it."

From beneath them, Dylan groaned.

"Hey, I think he's coming to," Chris said. "You there, buddy?" He asked Dylan as he lightly tapped his face.

Dylan opened his eyes.

"There he is," John said to him as if he was speaking to a baby waking up from a nap. "Welcome back, buddy."

"What happened?" He asked.

"You made it about three steps before you got bludgeoned to shit by one of the Watchers," Chris said.

"How many fingers am I holding up?" John said shoving his middle finger directly in Dylan's face.

"Fuck you too, man," Dylan said.

"What were you thinking, man?" Chris asked.

"Help me," Dylan said.

"I'm trying, man. Where does it hurt? What's wrong?"

"No, 'help me.' That girl had it carved into her neck, with a knife or something. She showed it to me."

"Seriously?" Chris asked. "You're sure you just don't have a concussion?"

"I'm serious," Dylan said rising to his feet. "We need to help her!"

Chapter 19

Lauren could not believe what had just happened. Did the one guy who might have helped her just get killed? How could he help her now if he was dead?

She walked slowly and began to realize this could be the last time she saw the surface. She felt the cool air on her cheeks and thought about how things were when she was alive. She thought about the things she would never see again. She thought about the way the air feels just before it's about to snow and the peace you feel when that first flake hits your face. She thought about summers on the shore and the feeling of nostalgia she used to feel when she heard the far-off crash of a wave.

She thought about Kevin. She wished she hadn't done what she did. The anger and the rage had overcome her that night, and she didn't even remember doing it. He had told her he had been unfaithful, and he confessed while she was far too close to that knife. She blacked out completely. When she came to, she had seen what she had done. And the horror of her crime was too much to bear. Her breast plate was the toughest part to get through. She didn't remember killing Kevin, but she remembered every second of what she did to herself.

A sick wash of despair started to rush back to her, as it always did at this point in the walk. She could feel the temperature of the air raise slightly and knew she was minutes away from being back in Hell, maybe for good this time.

She considered running, but it was too late. Watchers began fanning out in what they called "herding," keeping a tight perimeter, making sure no Walker had any room to run.

"Approaching the Entrance!" they yelled, as the Line slowed their pace and watchers emerged from different spots throughout.

Although Hell wasn't always the most tightly run ship, "herding" was an efficient operation, as Watchers grouped Walkers into tight groups of five or six and shoved them toward the entrance. Lauren felt the stern nudge of a Watchers' club push tightly into her back as they entered the narrow rock face that made up Hell's Front Porch. She shut her eyes tightly and felt the icy rush of permanent and eternal damnation.

Chapter 20

"You gotta take that suit off, man," Chris said to Dylan. "You're gonna get blood on it."

"After what I saw on the back of that girl's neck, I don't think it's something they watch too closely," Dylan said.
They were back at the Outer Shell, and Chris was tying a towel to Dylan's freshly battered head. John was scouring the break room fridge for snacks.
"What a weirdo," Chris said. "You sure you still want to pursue this chick. Seems like she's got issues."
"I think she's just desperate, man," Dylan said "What else was she gonna do? Write me an email? Damn it. Here comes a customer. You guys go hang on the side porch for a bit while I take care of this."
Chris and John walked to the side of the gift shop and exited out of the sliding door. In through the front door walked a man who was about 5'5" and easily over 300 pounds.
Dylan took one look at the man and thought of the term "symetrican," which was the term John had made up for people who are almost as wide as they are tall, making their symmetry line up in an almost perfect circle.
"How's it going, sir?" Dylan asked.
"Hey there, buddy, how you doing?" The man responded in a thick southern accent that made Dylan immediately gag.
"Pretty good. Let me know if I can help you with anything."
"Actually," the man began, "I was wondering if you could help me with some slot cars."
"Slot cars?" Dylan asked. "I'm not sure if I know what that is."

"You ain't never heard of slot cars? Oh man, they're pretty bitchin'. They're metal cars that line up on a track and go zipping all the way around the place. All the big hobby stores have 'em. Y'all don't carry 'em?"

"I'm almost positive we don't. I mean, we're not really a "hobby shop" per say, we're really more of a gift shop."

"What's the difference?" The man asked.

Dylan paused for a second. "Ya know, man, I'm not really too sure. I just know that we don't carry slot cars. We have a few t-shirts with cars on them though. See that one over there?" Dylan said motioning to a rack just to the left of the counter.

The symetrican walked over to the shirt, studied it carefully for a few moments and let out an eruption of laughter as he read the front of it."

"Hwy 90. The Highway to Hell. Literally. That's great, man! I'll take it! Y'all got XXL?"

"Of course we do," Dylan said. He really needed a change.

Chapter 21

Lawrence Thompson awoke to an eerie sound. He shot up quickly, certain he heard something that bounced him from a deep sleep. He remained motionless waiting to hear it again. He was breathless but heard nothing except the piercing still of the night and a few far-off passing cars. He was sure he had heard something. A voice perhaps?

After a few more seconds of silence, Lawrence assumed what he heard was nothing more than his imagination or an aftershock from a dream he had already forgotten. He put his head back on the pillow and was hoping to fall back asleep when he heard it again, and this time it was unmistakable. Someone was saying his name. "Lawrence," a dull voice whispered, sending shivers up his spine. He leapt from the comfort of his bed, tore across the room and flicked on the bedroom light.

"Who's there?" Lawrence asked.

No answer. Lawrence then went on a frantic tear through the house, turning on every light, swinging open all closet doors and picking up any object he thought he could use for a weapon. After settling on a meat tenderizer, Lawrence walked cautiously back in the direction of the bedroom to discover the source of the voice he had without a doubt heard.

"Where are you?" he shouted in the hallway between the bedroom and the guest bathroom.

"Up here, wanker," the voice said.

Lawrence shot his head upwards, expecting to see a deranged lunatic clinging from the ceiling like some sort of neurotic Spiderman, but nothing was there.

"Where?" he asked again.

"I'm in your head, ol' boy."

Lawrence had always secretly known this day would come. He had heard stories of other psychologists succumbing to the pressures of the job and eventually losing their minds. He just assumed it would happen later in life.

"Oh, I see. So you're not really here. You're all in my head. Well, if you're in my head, what am I thinking right now?"

"How the bloody hell should I know what you're thinking?" the voice responded. "Probably something about how your mother didn't hug you enough growing up, ya bloomin' onion!"

Lawrence wondered why he had invented a split personality that was so aggressive. Perhaps it was a response to how passively he handled things in his personal life. He also wondered why the voice in his head had such a bad British accent.

"Well, what do you want? What can I do for you?"

"You have to let him die, ol' boy. It's the only way."

"Let who die? Mr. Rainbow?"

"Who the bloody 'ell is Mr. Rainbow?" the voice asked.

"He's my hamster. He's been sick for a while and the vet suggested…"

"You think I give a fuck about your hamster?" The voice angrily interrupted. "I'm talking about David Estern."

"David Estern, the inmate?"

"You know another one?"

"I guess not," Lawrence said. "What do you want with Estern?"

"Let's just say we have some plans for him, some rather large ones. If you do what you're told, maybe we can help you. But in order for any of this to happen, you need to let the warden and the rest of his cronies know that David is as fit as a fiddle and ready to be executed in any way you see fit. That way, he can come down here and join the rest of us."

"But he's not sane. He hears voices. He talks to them."

"And just what do you think you're doing right now?

"Good point," Lawrence said. "Are you the one who talks to David? You told him to do those awful things?"

"Yes I did, Lawrence. It's all part of the plan."

"What plan? Who are you?"

"Down here they call me the Dragon."

"Whaoh, cool name."

"Shut it! Now let's discuss how you are going to help our little plan come along and how much pain you'll feel if you get in my way…"

When Lawrence got up the next day, he tried convincing himself that he wasn't crazy. He had spoken to the voice in his head for nearly an hour that night, the voice with the inexplicable British accent that told him to execute David Estern.

The Dragon claimed to be a high ranking official in Hell and insisted that they needed people like Estern and himself to carry out "the master plan." Lawrence didn't think he could make up things like this. He wasn't creative enough. Lawrence was aware of the existence of Hell Exits all throughout the country and was mildly fascinated with the phenomena they represented, but he had always considered himself to be a nonbeliever. He was one of the many people who believed that the dark cavern openings were nothing more than that, and the people who walked were just a bunch of freaks. He had always thought people were crazy for believing the Exits had supernatural powers. He equated it to the lady who saw Jesus in a grilled cheese sandwich. That lady and everyone who believed in Hell, were bat-shit crazy. So what was he?

He started to think about the possibility that maybe he wasn't crazy. That maybe the Dragon was real and he really did speak to him and maybe he really spoke to David Estern as well. If this was the case and Estern was not crazy either, then this meant that he could be executed, like the Dragon wanted. Just to be safe, Lawrence felt it was best not to argue with the voice inside his head.

Even if Estern was totally nuts, was it worth sparing his life if it meant a lifetime of haunting from an English ghost with a really cool nick name? Besides, the piece of shit had killed a child. Lawrence decided that, crazy or not, he was going to do everything in his power to make sure David Estern would pay for his crimes and be sent to the cold, black bowels of Hell where he belonged.

Chapter 22

"Bang up job, blokes! Really stellar work!" Gregory Irons said to Daman and Neville Black. The three of them were all sitting on top of Inhabitants who were on their hands and knees, their limbs twitching with strain. "I can just feel it. The hope is being completely sucked out of this place. I mean just look at these two sorry excuses for humans," Irons said motioning to the people under Daman's and Neville's butts."

"We seet on them," Daman said. "They are like furniture."
"Brilliant, just brilliant," Irons said. "Attention to detail gentlemen. It's little things like this that make this place just that much more miserable. This is just brilliant."
"Thank you, sir," Mr. Black responded, shifting on his groaning Inhabitant. "Daman thought it was a nice touch."
Daman nodded and smiled, but did not speak as he was eating a sandwich and thought it was impolite to speak with his mouth full. Although it was Neville's idea to start sitting on the Inhabitants, he always gave credit to Daman. He knew the importance of keeping Daman happy and also knew, in case of an uprising, it was best to not let the Inhabitants be too upset with the guy who just took orders.
"What else have you done with the place?" the Dragon asked.
"Well, you're probably noticing it's a bit brighter down here," Neville said looking pleased with himself.
"Is it?" Irons asked.
"I would hope so," Neville continued. "We've raised the wattage on all incandescent bulbs from a mildly irritating 70 watts to a near blinding 80. It's really quite uncomfortable."

"Ah yes," Irons said as he looked upwards toward the lighting. "I guess it is a little different and a tad more irritating. I guess I see the effect. What else, though? Where's the pain? Are we still letting people take their little vacations to the surface whenever they please?"

"Surface passes are down nearly 50%, and the Line gets smaller and smaller every day. It's more like a surface fragment now," Neville joked.

"Good one, ol' boy," Irons said dryly. "While we're on the subject of people leaving, though, let's also talk about the amount of people we're bringing in. We need more like-minded people down here, more people who get it. People like us. "

"Like me?" Daman asked through a mouthful of ham salad.

"Yes, ol' boy. People just like you. Ruthless people, evil people, people who will revel in the fire and flame and bask in the sulfuric nightmare that people have come to expect of this place. People who can give out a good lashing and take pleasure in doing so.

"Excuse me for interrupting," Neville said, "but we have no control over who comes down here. People are sentenced here based on things they have done on Earth. We have nothing to do with that. People just show up through the portal. How do we control what people do when they're living."

Irons hadn't told either of them what he had been doing with people like David Estern, and he was not planning on telling them. He didn't want them to know that his ultimate plan did not include them, and, when the time was right, he would dethrone them. In the meantime, he would lie to them and make them think nothing was wrong.

"Oh, I suppose you're bloody right," Irons said. "Well, I guess we'll just hope the right blokes show up. Cheerio."

Gregory gave a quick nod to each of them and walked away. An insidious smile formed on his lips. He knew the right people were showing up and would be there very soon. Soon, he would rule them all. No one would ever laugh at Steven Arby ever again.

Chapter 23

Dylan was finishing his shift and was out back emptying the trash in the dumpster behind Outer Shell. He still had his orange jumpsuit on. He was too tired to take it off.

John and Chris had gone home, but they had made plans to meet at Reevers for drinks and to discuss their next plan of action. Dylan didn't know what he was going to do. Twice now he had tried to get into Hell, and twice he had failed. He shook his head in disgust, opened the lid to the dumpster and was set to throw the heavy bag into it when a noise from behind startled him. He turned to see a shabby, presumably homeless man, rifling through a nearby dumpster, looking for whatever discarded remnants he could add to his shopping cart, piled high with survival items.

"How's it going?" Dylan said not wanting to be rude.

The man lifted his head from the dumpster and gave a nod before continuing with his previously designated task.

"I think there's some cans in here," he said motioning to the bag. "I mean, they're empty, but maybe you can turn them in and get some cash for them."

"What do you mean?" the man asked. "Like a reward? Are those cans wanted for murder?"

Taken aback by the man's callous humor, Dylan let out a nervous laugh.

"No, ha. I mean, like recycling money. People still do that, right?"

"Not sure Captain Planet," the man said. "Haven't read this month's *Better Homes and Gardens*. You can hang onto your cans though, fella. I'll be just fine."

The man turned away from Dylan and began rifling through the crowded dumpster again, seemingly forgetting Dylan was standing there.

"Oh, excuuuse me!" Dylan said. "Sorry for trying to help you, man. At least I'm talking to you. Half the people around here don't give people like you the time of day."

"People like me?" The man said, walking over to Dylan before stopping just short of him. "What does that mean, people like me? Do you mean the Irish or people named Brian or do you mean bums?"

Dylan swallowed hard, knowing that the man was most likely seconds away from losing his temper.

"No, man. I mean...come on. I was only trying to help."

"You work here?" The man said motioning towards the Outer Shell.

"Yeah," Dylan said.

The man surveyed the outside of the building in mock interest before finally rolling his eyes and letting out a condescending snort.

"Looks like you need help more than I do, buddy. Nice suit by the way." The man retrieved his shopping cart and walked away from Dylan, up the alley and into the street.

Dylan stood motionless in the alley for a few moments before looking down at the leaking bag of garbage at his feet. He had been taking out the trash to the same dirty dumpster for the past eleven years. In that time period, all he had to show for it was a thousand hangovers, ten thousand pointless conversations, two near fist fights with customers and the lingering and debilitating effects of a broken heart. Now, when he was most vulnerable, a man covered in dirt and urine had just scoffed at his very existence.

Dylan dropped the bag of garbage in the alley without putting it in the dumpster and walked away towards the street, away from

Outer Shell. When he hit the street, he looked back at the store's lifeless visage burning a life-sucking shadow over his hometown. He decided he was no longer going to work there. He didn't lock the door or pull the shutters over the windows and felt no remorse as he walked away from the store and onto the street.

Had he known it would be one of his last moments on Earth, he might have gone back for a t-shirt.

Dylan joined Chris and John at Reevers and immediately told them the news about his job. He started drinking as soon as he walked away from the Outer Shell, buying four 24 oz. cans of Miller Hi-Life from the closest liquor store and drinking them on the front porch of his apartment complex – taking massive swigs and staring listlessly into the street. Now at the bar, it was clear the alcoholic onslaught was not about to stop.

"So you're just gonna quit?" John asked.

"I already did," Dylan said. "Let's get some shots," he said, turning to find an available waitress.

"Well, did you tell anybody?" Chris asked, "Did you even leave a note telling your boss you wouldn't be back?"

"No," Dylan said. "In fact I'm pretty sure I didn't even lock the door. Actually I know I didn't. Whoops!"

The three of them shared a laugh.

"That's great, man," John said. "Now you can start working with me!"

"No offense, John," Chris said. "But I'm actually surprised that you work. What exactly is it you do?"

"Of course I work, man," John said. "I started my own company. I'm a consultant."

"Consultant for what?" Chris asked.

"I'm a Crass consultant."

"A Crass consultant?" Chris asked.

"Yeah, man," John said sitting up straight in his chair. "Have you ever seen a commercial or an advertising campaign where someone just misses something overtly sexual?"

"I'm not sure I follow," Chris said. "Give me an example."

"OK," John said thinking for a second. "The Flex-A-Bell."

"That thing that women use to get fat off their arms?" Chris asked. "What about it?"

"Well, it's no secret that that thing looks like girls are giving a serious hand job when they're using that thing. It's a joke. It's become a party gag that people give away at bachelorette parties."

"Sure, I get that," Chris said. "But where do you come in?"

"It's my job as a Crass consultant to stop those things before they get too far. Had Flex-A-Bell hired me, I would have told them it looked like a cock being jerked off and they coulda tweaked the model or at least changed the commercials."

"And what qualifies you to make these observations?" Chris asked.

"I'm the classic every man. Plus I like dick and fart jokes. Corporate people are too detached from reality. They need someone like me."

"And has anyone hired your services yet, or is this still a start up?"

"Still kinda getting off the ground, but I've been talking to the creators of the Unicorn Headband to try to get them to see the light. It's a headband that kids wear on the top of their head that totally looks like a…"

"Yeah, yeah, I get it," Chris interrupted.

"I'm at least trying to get them to change their slogan, 'Strap on the Fun.' It's baffling how much they've overlooked."

"You're a real pillar to the community," Chris said.

"Thanks, man," John said.

"Well John," Dylan began, "as much as I appreciate the offer of the job, I think I'm gonna pass. But you're doing it, man. It's something to be proud of."

"It is?" Chris asked.

"Hell yeah, it is!" Dylan slurred. "He's following his dreams, and soon he's gonna achieve his goals. Something I will never, ever do."

"Of course you will, man. You're just in a rough patch," Chris said.

"A rough patch? My whole life has been a rough patch. Do you know the most amazing thing that ever happened to me happened when I was seven years old?"

"Not the t-ball thing?" John groaned.

"Yeah, John, the t-ball thing! That was supposed to be a premonition of things to come. It was supposed to show me how great things were gonna be for me, and instead every moment after that has been total….phhhhhht."

"What happened?" Chris asked.

"You really don't want to hear it, dude," John said. "He tells this story all of the time."

"Yeah, he wants to hear it," Dylan said. "He needs to hear this."

"I really do," Chris said.

"Like I said, I was seven years old and, also, like I said, I was playing t-ball. You know how in t-ball there are always like fifty kids on a team so when you're out in the field they just scatter you everywhere. There's no positions or anything. It's just wherever they can find room for you, right?"

"It's been awhile since I watched a t-ball game, but I get what you're saying," Chris said.

"There are kids everywhere. So the coach puts me in the infield, real close to the plate, like in front of the pitchers mound – way too close for a gangly kid like me. Most of the game, everything is fine. Some little dweeby kid makes light contact with the ball, it dribbles about five feet in front of the plate and then all fifty kids go sprinting after it. No actual plays are made. But then things got scary: Ralph Briggs comes up to the plate."

"Who's that?" Chris asked.

"Oh, every kid grew up with a Ralph Briggs, the kid who's a foot taller than everyone else and starts growing facial hair at the age of five, the kid everyone was afraid of."

"So he comes up to bat," Chris prompted.

"Yeah, Ralph comes up to bat. This massive kid, who is probably as big as I am now, comes up to bat and I'm standing like 15 feet away, just waiting for him to tattoo one right at my Adam's apple. I'm a sitting duck. So rather than just move back like a sensible person, I decide my best plan of attack is to close my eyes."

"You close your eyes?" Chris asked.

"Yeah, like a fucking ostrich, I figure if I don't see it, it's not really happening. So I close my eyes. But then something tells me while I'm at it to hold my glove out, just in case. I swear this wasn't my decision, something made the decision for me. So I stick both arms out, like I'm Jesus fucking Christ just waiting for the sound of bat on ball and then…wham."

"Wham?" Chris asked.

"Wham," replied Dylan.

"So it hit you? Where did the ball hit you?"

"Right in the glove. I fucking caught it. Eyes closed, arms out, the ball gets hit and sticks directly in my glove. No one on the team knew I had my eyes closed, so they just figured it was a nice catch by a rising young athlete. But I know it was a miracle."

"I don't know if I'd call it that, more like an impressive coincidence," said John.

"It was a miracle," Dylan corrected. "A miracle that was supposed to tell me everything was gonna be OK, but I messed it up somehow, like I mess up everything else in my life."

"Look man, it's been a long day," Chris began. "Let's back off the sad topics and try to have some fun. We can get back to trying to sneak back into the Line another time."

"It's all sad, homie," Dylan said before knocking back another shot of whiskey. "The happy times are just moments where it hasn't gone to shit yet. I gotta go take a piss," Dylan said before walking past the bathrooms and out of the front door.

"He knows people don't like to have their cars peed on, right?" Chris asked.

"Oh, he's fine man. He just stepped out to get some fresh air. He'll be right back."

Chapter 24

"So you think he's totally bullshitting everybody?" warden Dormeus asked Lawrence Thompson. "You honestly believe that?"

The two were seated across from each other at the prison staff cafeteria. Lawrence was drinking a chai latte and the warden was enjoying his fourth cup of black coffee. Lawrence had just told the warden, in light of the Dragon's coaxing, that he felt that David Estern was completely fit to be executed and that they should move forward with the process as soon as humanly possible. Lawrence tried to make his pitch to the warden sound as sincere as he could, but his voice still trembled as he spoke as he was terrified that the Dragon was listening, hidden somewhere in the caverns of his mind.

"Oh yeah," he said. "That guy is messing with us. He's just trying to save his own ass. We ran a series of neurological tests on him, and there's nothing that suggests any sort of trauma or deficiencies. I say we fry this asshole and make sure that doesn't happen."

"Why Mr. Thompson, when did you become Mr. Capital Punishment? I thought you were like governor Corzine and the rest of those hippies who worked towards rehabilitating these scum bags? Good to know you're finally seeing the light."

"I just think it's applicable here, sir. What Estern did is unforgivable."

"OK, Lawrence, I'm with you then. I'll go ahead and give the right people a call and let them know what we've decided. They'll be happy to hear it. Is there someone you need to contact as well?"

"Maybe one person," Lawrence said thinking about the Dragon.

"But I'm guessing he already knows."

Lawrence Thompson was speeding down the corridor of death row, racing to talk to David Estern. He realized he had never been so excited to tell someone he was going to be executed. He blew past every person he saw on the jog over without even saying hello and stopped at Estern's cell. He was asleep in his bunk. He unlocked the receiving door quickly.

"David," Lawrence whispered, glancing over his shoulder. The guard, who was about 10 feet away from them had his feet up on a desk and was reading a copy of *XXL* magazine. Since PHP, the guards who remained on staff seemed to give even less of a shit about their jobs.

"David," he tried again. Still nothing.

"David Estern, wake the fuck up!" Lawrence finally yelled, causing Estern to shoot up quickly from his sleep and the guard to look up from his magazine.

"Gotta be tough with these whackos," Lawrence said to the guard who responded by burying his face back in his magazine.

"Jesus Christ, Thompson. You scared the shit out of me," Estern said.

"Sorry," he responded.

"What do you want," Estern said, rubbing his eyes and sitting upright on the edge of his bed.

"I have great news," Lawrence whispered. "You're going to die, we're gonna kill you and it's all because of me. I did what he told me to do."

"What who told you to do?" Estern asked.

"You know…him, the Dragon. He spoke to me."

David rose slowly from his bed and walked over to the door. He knelt down so his face was in the opening receiving door and prompted Lawrence to do the same. The two were face to face.

Lawrence realized he had never been this close to a deranged psycho path before.

"He spoke to you too, huh? So I'm not crazy?"

"No, you're totally sane. I get it now. He explained everything. That's why the state decided they can kill you, with my recommendation. Isn't that great?"

David shot a quick hand through the door and grabbed Lawrence by his shirt, pulling him violently towards the door. The guard glanced up from his magazine but still refused to leave his seat.

"Hey, what's going on over there?"

"Nothing, nothing, everything's fine," Lawrence responded. "All part of the treatment. Just an anger management exercise."

"Fucking hippie," the guard mumbled and returned to his magazine.

"What is wrong with you?" Lawrence whispered "I thought you'd be happy?"

"Happy?" David pulled hard on his collar again, causing Lawrence to hit his head on the metal door with a resounding clang. The guard just sighed and shook his head.

"Listen to me, you little shit," David said. "Nothing, since this whole thing began two years ago, has made me happy. It has been a living nightmare and I know I'll never get over what I've done. Now you're telling me that I'm going to die and I'm supposed to be happy?"

"But...it's all going according to plan. The Dragon said he'd take care of us both if we do what he says. We have nothing to worry about."

"Ya know, when I first heard the voice and I did what I did, I thought the same as you," David said finally letting go of Lawrence's shirt. "I trusted the voice and in some strange way I thought I was doing the right thing. I felt safe. But since then, the voice stopped talking to me and I'm starting to lose that feeling of comfort. I can feel a new voice creeping in. Not as loud and apparent as the Dragon's voice, but something buried in my conscience. It's telling me I was wrong. It's making me think about that day and about the people I hurt, the lives I ruined. It's telling me that I was tricked."

"No," Thompson demanded. "It can't be. Why would he trick us?"

"Because that's what evil does, Lawrence. It tricks you into doing what it wants and then it throws you away. I don't know where I'm going after this life ends, I just know it will be dark and wicked and any feeling of hope or security I thought I once had will never find me again."

Chapter 25

The portal that transported in-coming Inhabitants to Hell opened roughly every 20 minutes. Peoples' souls, when sentenced to Hell, left their physical bodies on Earth and were shot through the portal unexpectedly and directly into Hell. One minute, you are flipping your car over on an icy road or putting a gun to your head in a final act of protest and then bam! You are suddenly in a different realm, transported into a world of menacing demons screaming obscenities at you, the smell of rotting corpses and the deafening pop of fire erupting through every corner of the walls.

A scene like this is not typical of the rest of the underworld. The rest of the underworld is pretty mundane, focusing more on the reality of eternity and less on supernatural terrors. But at Hell's portal and entrance, grand presentations like this are used to stir terror into the hearts of arriving Inhabitants. The show that took place at the portal was a 23 hour a day exhibition, with an hour break in between so the Inhabitants dressed as demons could take off their suits and use the bathroom.

The time in between the actual death and the transport into Hell only lasts about two minutes. Those two minutes are the only time a soul ever truly ceases to be. This time in purgatory has been argued by philosophers to be the only time when a person truly is free. Jason Dunam, author of the book *Your Soul and You*, theorized that the sensation was similar to the time he got to throw out the first pitch at a New York Yankees spring training game in Tampa, FL. Similar statements helped ensure the book went on to only sell 300 copies worldwide.

Before and after the two minutes of actual death, the following sequence occurs to a human body during the death process:

1. **Panic:** An overwhelming sense of panic sets in as your system senses something is wrong.

2. **Calming:** A tranquil state is reached as your body and brain shut down.

3. **Numbness:** The calm turns to incapacitating relaxation and your vision starts to tunnel.

4. **Bowel release:** Yes, this really does happen.

5. Death: The period of blackness where the soul floats to its final destination, either upwards or downwards.

6. **Reawakening:** The soul begins to reassemble in physical form, brain retains original function.

7. **Transport:** The newly reformed body is transported through a portal to either a) Heaven for the good. b) Hell for the bad c) Reincarnation for the marginal.

Gregory Irons, Neville Black and Daman were standing by the portal, waiting for it to open to greet the next Inhabitant. This was far from a normalcy, as usually Inhabitants were anything but greeted. Usually, upon stepping out of the blinding light, which Hell uses as a trick to make people think they were going to Heaven, new Inhabitants are doused in near boiling water, beaten and ridiculed for their unsightly naked appearance. They are then forced to put on the Hell-mandated orange jumpsuit before being given a series of painful, purple nurples and Indian Burns.

The physical abuse was second fiddle, though, to the verbal barbs thrown at the Inhabitants. Hell greeters were trained on how to locate someone's insecurities and had a myriad of ways to make the person feel awful about it. An Inhabitant with a little extra fat around their belly would be sure to hear some crack about the lack of jelly doughnuts in Hell, while a very skinny Inhabitant would get some sort of lunch meat shoved in their mouths. It was quite cruel.

On this day, however, Irons was hoping to introduce Daman and Mr. Black to an incoming member whose arrival was personally orchestrated by Irons. The Dragon had not let them know this was his doing and just claimed that he had heard about it by checking the arrival sheet in the counselor's office.

"This guy is great," Irons began. "Tommy Shareef. He was recently proven solely responsible for the death of seventeen people. Fortunately for us, he was one of the deceased. I am quite proud of myself for the crime I made him do."

"The crime You made him do, sir," Neville asked.

"What? Er, no, sorry, slip of the tongue, ol' boy. A wag of the ol' wonker, as we used to say back in England. I, of course, meant the thing I heard he did. I had nothing to do with it. How could I?" Irons had not been entirely careful with hiding his plan and had been slipping up like this a lot recently, but he knew that Daman and Neville were too stupid to figure out what was going on.

"So what did he do?" Neville asked. "What is bringing him here?"

"Let's just say this native of Allentown made a huge splash on his 23rd birthday," Irons said, pausing for a moment, waiting for recognition from the other two.

"Go on," Neville said. "Big splash, 23rd birthday...what happened next?."

"Allentown? Big splash? Crickey, don't you two have any clue what goes on up there?"

Daman and Mr. Black turned towards each other and shrugged.

"The Allentown flood? The Allentown dam busted and killed a bunch of geezers. Ring any bells?"

"Ah, yes, de flood. De big one. I see now," Daman said despite not knowing what Iron's was referencing.

"Tommy was the one that pulled the plug, and 64 tons of c4 and the whole thing went pop. The kid's a genius, and he'll be here any minute. He'll be all ours."

"What is he gonna do for us?" Neville asked.

"Anything we want, ol' boy," Irons said.

Chapter 26

Dylan had just relieved himself outside of the bar and was struggling to get back into his orange suit. He swayed in large, swooping loops, moving further and further away from the bar with each inebriated swipe. Back and forth, he stumbled and wandered away from the blinding lights and familiar chatter of the bar and into the soothing blackness of the woods nearby. He finally righted himself by holding onto a tree and finalized the otherwise simple act of clothing himself. He pulled at the bright fabric, trying to straighten himself up, when he noticed his pocket was shaking. It took him several seconds before he finally realized his cell phone was ringing.

He dug into his pocket, retrieved the phone and squinted at the screen. It read "Woodhouse," the clinic where his mother went for therapy. She was calling again. Dylan sighed, realizing that this was the absolute worst time to answer the phone, but rationalized that he was better equipped to deal with his mother's rants when he was shit faced.

"Hey, mom," he said into the phone trying not to slur his words to bad.

"Dylan?" the voice on the other end said.

"Yeah, who's this?"

"Dylan, it's Lilly."

"Who?" Dylan asked.

"It's Lilly, Dylan, your mother's pathologist."

"Oh shit!" Dylan shouted before lowering his voice again. "Er, I mean. Lilly, what's going on? You thinking twice about getting that drink? Come meet me. I'm at Reevers , close by it anyway."

"I can't, Dylan."

"Ahhhh, come on!"

"Dylan I need you to listen to me. It's about your mother. I don't know how to tell you this, but she passed, Dylan. She'd dead."

Dylan felt a shift in the air. His ears clogged up like he was ascending in an airplane. Something was collapsing on top of him and he was being crushed.

"She's what?"

"She's dead, Dylan. She didn't show up for her appointment today, and they found her in her apartment. She had taken some pills."

"She killed herself?"

"They don't know, Dylan. They're still trying to find that out. They only found her a few hours ago. I'm sorry I have to be the one to tell you this. I just wanted it to be from someone you know. Are you OK?"

"She's been trying to call me," Dylan said. "She was trying to tell me something."

"This has nothing to do with you, Dylan. Don't start thinking like that."

"She was asking for help and I ignored her. I'm a horrible son. I did this."

"No Dylan, please don't…" Lilly's voice began to waver, and she started to cry on the other end of the line.

"I'm a horrible person. I…" Dylan stopped in mid-sentence, the temperature dropped and he was shaking. His ears blocked out the sounds of bar chatter and began to pinhole into a high pitched ring like the sound of a TV left on in an otherwise quiet room. He dropped the phone and accepted the dying cry that pulsed in his head.

"Dylan? Hello? Dylan?" Lilly shouted through the phone that now lay on the leaf-covered ground. Dylan heard nothing. A small line of blood shot from his nostril. His old friend.

Dylan's vision began to tunnel. What started as a flashing light in the corners of his eyes closed in on his corneas, creating a relaxing blanket of nothingness that completely blinded him. Alone and senseless, standing at the break of a dark woods, Dylan's body had become an empty vessel, devoid of any human emotion. It was hollow. Dylan James was, for the moment, somewhere else, but his body began to move. Something beckoned to it. A nameless force shook the body from its standing point and pushed it deeper into the woods. Efficient and determined, Dylan's body walked through the blackness of the Brinton woods towards a destination that had previously eluded him. The Underworld was calling to the hopeless and seemingly lifeless body of Dylan James. It was ready to welcome him in. Dylan's brain had become a slide show, emitting flashing memories of his life. It was a carnival of changing colors as his brain caught fleeting glimpses of shades of black, gray and white. His body was trying to awaken his brain, but his brain resisted. His body, however, was alive and well. Determined and persistent, it carried itself through the thick woods. The body's legs quickened their pace to a slow jog while the body's arms were resting straight and unbending at its sides, like a zombie attempting to river dance.

One hundred yards ahead, the faint shuffle of feet could be heard as hundreds of undead beings marched back into their final place of rest.

The body stretched its legs and began to sprint. Faster than Dylan himself had ever run before, the body carried itself around a clearing of trees where the Line from Hell marched stoically, barely visible by the yellow crescent moon that hung high in the sky.

The body steadied its pace, remaining slightly ahead of the

cadence the Walkers were keeping before slowing just at the back of the Line. The body then slid ever so slightly to its right and slipped into order, like the final puzzle piece snapping in.

The Line accepted Dylan's body as its own. A faint haze crept into Dylan's head and he smelled something familiar – cold? Can you smell cold?

From the colorful haze, a small black dot appeared in the center, and, as it opened wider, something emerged from it. Easy Money, stepped out of the haze, again looking as dapper as ever with tuxedo, top hat, cane and all.

"You again?" Dylan asked.

"Yeah, mother fucka, me again. Guardian angel, remember? I got this shit on lock down." Easy answered. "Well, well, well, look at you now. Looks like you finally did it."

"I did what?" Dylan asked.

"Do you know where you at right now? You're almost there, bitch, marching right up to the entrance to Hell without a care in the world. Think about it, Dylan. You really want this?"

"No, I know where I am," Dylan protested. "I'm at a bar and I'm fucking wasted. I am outside talking to Lilly. Oh shit, my mom is dead."

"No reason to bitch about that now, my man. She's closer than you think."

"What do you mean? She's dead. I'll never see her again."

"Let me ask you this again. Do you know where you're at right now? She's getting closer with each step you take. Keep that head up, baby. We're gonna miss you up here."

"Uh yeah, later. Where are you going?"

"Back to the store, bitch. I got kids to feed! Goodbye, Dylan. Ala-fucking-kazam," Easy said, tapping his cane on the ground in front of him. It made a much louder sound than it rightfully should have, and the smack jarred Dylan awake.

The first thing he heard was the sound of a far off fire. He was walking straight towards it.

Chapter 27

"The art of sneaking?" Chris asked. "You just follow people around and hope they don't call the cops on you?"

"At its base, yeah, but there's more to it than that. It's a practice in human behavior. People do some strange things when they think no one's watching. They do even stranger things when they find out someone *is* watching. I'll send you a link, man. I think you'd be into it."

"I think I've heard all I need to know, John. Thanks though."

Chris had been listening to John talk about his various sneaking adventures for 20 minutes. As moronic as they were, they were easy to get wrapped up in. He realized in those 20 minutes that Dylan had not come back inside of the bar after drunkenly wandering out of it.

"He's been gone kind of a long time, don't you think?" Chris asked.

"Dylan? I guess so. I assumed he was just smoking a cigarette or talking to a girl. He'll be back soon. So this one time, I was following this waiter from the Olive Garden…"

"Let's go look for him," Chris interrupted.

The two finished what was left of their drinks and walked out of the bar to look for Dylan. Outside of the bar, there were a few drunk women talking way too loud, but Dylan was not with them.

"It's called *Pimp My Ride,*" one of the girls shouted. "It's so cool! Xzibit is the host. I think he's so fucking hot."

"Excuse me," Chris said to them. "Sorry to interrupt, but have you seen a really drunk guy wandering around here? He's wearing a bright orange jumpsuit."

"Oh my God, I love your hair!" Drunk girl #2 shouted. "How do you get it like that?"

"I just get it cut," Chris said, "with scissors and a razor."

"That's so cool!"

"Yeah, I guess so. So, you haven't seen our friend? He's hard to miss."

"Sorry, darling, not since we've been out here."

"Thanks," Chris said, walking away from the two girls and motioning for John to follow him on a perimeter search of the bar.

"I really wouldn't worry about him," John said. "He does this a lot. He's famous for wandering off when he gets drunk and somehow ending up back in his bed."

Chris then heard a strange noise coming from the woods at the back of a bar, a persistent racket that he couldn't place at first.

"What's that?" Chris asked John.

John listened for a second and said, "Sounds like someone left a phone off the hook."

The two walked back into the woods and found the source of the sound, Dylan's cell phone lying on the ground, still open and insistently beeping.

"Is that Dylan's?" Chris asked

John bent over and picked it up, closing it and stopping the noise. "Yeah, it definitely is. See this sticker remnant on the back? It used to be a Bouncing Souls sticker that he put on there when he first got the phone. It must've fallen out of his pocket or something? Where the fuck is he though? Do you think he got kidnapped?"

"Kidnapped?" Chris asked. "Who the hell would want to kidnap Dylan? You think there's a big ransom for broke, 30-year-old white dudes?"

"Then where did he go?"

Something dawned on Chris. He walked further behind the bar and saw the worn down path caused by Travelers. The Line had probably walked through here very recently.

"What time is it?" John asked

"It's 10:15," John answered, after looking at his phone.

Chris had a pretty good handle on the Line's schedule and knew that the late-night Line usually started at 10:00. Judging by their current location, it was entirely feasible that the Line had passed by the bar within the hour. It was close enough that a drunken buffoon with an inferiority complex could've been drawn to it.

"You don't think he..." Chris began. "There's no way he...Are you thinking what I'm thinking?"

"Gypsys?" John asked.

"The Line, man! Do you think he tried to get into the Line again?"

"The Line?" John said. "Oh, crap! The Line! I bet that's exactly where he went."

"I think if we follow this path we can catch up to him! We gotta go before he gets the shit beat out of him again. This time he may actually be killed."

"Let's go then! But can I hold the binoculars this time?"

"Hurry!" Chris said before grabbing John by the coat sleeve and dragging him into the forest. They wandered through the woods desperately looking for Dylan.

"We're fucking lost, dude," John said to Chris as the two of them crept through the pines.

"We are not," Chris insisted. "I've made this trip dozens of times before." Chris stopped and surveyed their surroundings. "We may be back-tracking a tad, tough."

"Back-tracking? That sounds like lost to me. If you've been here dozens of times how do you not know where we're going?"

"Well, I would usually follow the Line during the day. At night everything looks the same."

"Oh man, remind me to never get directions from you. I'll be trying to get to Hackensack and end up in China."

"In what? Your floating fucking car?"

"Yeah, that's right, in my floating car that I'm going to invent and make millions of dollars, and you're not going to get any it because you're…"

"Wait!" Chris interrupted.

"What?"

"Do you hear that?"

From the silence of the night a slow muffled sound began to rise, a faint crackling sound.

"Yeah. What is that?" John asked.

"We're here." Chris whispered. "We have to be quiet."

Chris slowly crept towards the crackling sound and John followed. With each silent step the sound grew louder. The two reached the top of a hill, and, while crouching down, peered over the edge. The Line from Hell was being herded into a gaping hole that emitted a dull orange glow. About thirty Walkers were left, and they were going quickly. Dylan was one of them.

"Oh man, is this it?" John asked.

"This is it," Chris said.

"Do you see him?"

Chris squinted his eyes, hoping to catch a glimpse of Dylan through the darkness, hoping the faint glow from the rock face would help his cause. After five more walkers entered through the hole, Chris saw Dylan.

"There he is. I see him. He's at the back of the herd. There are about twenty people ahead of him."

"Well we have to do something!" John said shooting up from his crouch.

"What do you mean? This is what he wanted."

"It's not safe. We need to be there with him."

"It's too late. There's nothing we can do."

"Fuck that!" John yelled. Chris could see what John was about to do and grabbed his foot while he attempted to run down to Dylan. John tripped while attempting to step, but caught himself with his hands.

"Let go of me!" he screamed as he tried to kick loose of Chris's grasp.

"You can't run down there. They'll kill you!"

"I don't care. He's my friend. I need to help him!"

Fifty yards ahead of them, unaware of his friend's epic struggle, Dylan was passing from the Earth into the entrance of Hell. Being the last Walker through the Entrance, the three remaining Watchers surveyed the entrance to make sure everyone was accounted for and no living people were around. They walked into Hell's entrance as the giant stone door slowly slid shut behind them, sealing off the underworld from Earth and leaving the Brinton woods in silence.

Up on the hill, the battle raged on.

"You give up?" Chris asked John while holding him in an inescapable headlock.

"You're gonna regret this, man. I wrestled in junior high," John said as the lower half of his body twisted and contorted as he attempted to free his upper half.

Chris let out a quick giggle before he then realized he had been so wrapped up in wrestling this moron that he had not been watching the Line. He looked down towards the entrance and saw that everyone was gone.

"Oh no," he said loosening his grip on John's head.

John used the opportunity to free his head. He then shoved Chris down to the ground, jumping on top of him and pinning his shoulders to the ground. Chris did not resist at all.

"One, two, three! Gotcha, bitch! John Tate is the champion once again!"

"Would you get the hell off me and look. Dylan is gone, man. They all are."

"What?" John said as he jumped off of Chris and looked in the direction of the entrance.

All that remained was a small spiral of smoke ascending from the jagged rocks.

"Where did they go?" John asked.

"Where do you think? They went down there."

"Whoa, that's heavy."

"Yeah, it is," Chris said as he rose and dusted himself off. He walked over to John and the two of them looked down at the entrance of Hell.

"I don't think we thought this through," John said. "I think he's in real trouble."

"For once I agree with you. We have to do something."

"But what?" John asked.

Chris shook his head in disbelief, realizing the enormity and severity of the situation. "We have to get in there. We have to follow him and we have to get him out of there."

"What's the plan?" John asked.

Chris thought about the circumstances surrounding Dylan's successful entrance into Hell. Dylan was very drunk the last time they saw him. Maybe there was something to that.

"Do you have your flask on you, John?" he asked.

"Always," John said pulling it from his back pocket and dangling it in the air.

"How full is it?"

"To the brim."

"We need to figure out a plan and I think it starts with us finishing that flask."

"Now you're speaking my language," John said opening the flask and taking a long pull before passing it to Chris who did the same. The two sat on the forest floor determined to get as drunk as the contents of the flask could get them and hoped that answers would somehow come to them.

Chapter 28

As he entered the underworld, Dylan was greeted by pure madness. His ears shook with the droning sound of a siren that rattled the air. Every time he thought his eyes were ready to see something, an explosion of light burrowed through his pupils and disoriented him. He could only see shapes and some of them shoved him forward every time he tried to stop to see where he was. It was so hot. The air singed the hairs on his arms and stung the back of his eyes. Flames shot out of the walls and nipped at his heels.

He heard loud voices forcing their way through the sound of the siren but couldn't make out what they were saying. He looked around, and, jammed into the rock walls with no rhyme or reason, were hundreds of television sets. Some were tuned to static and were emitting the sounds of white noise while others were tuned into commercials, selling products at an obnoxiously loud volume. "FOR A LIMITED TIME ONLY, WHEN YOU PURCHASE ONE SUIT, GET ANOTHER ONE OF EQUAL OR LESSER VALUE FOR FREE..."
"THE FORD F-150, NOW WITH MORE TOWING CAPACITY THAN EVER BEFORE..."
"IF YOU FIND A BETTER DEAL AT ANY STORE IN THE CITY, I WILL SLAP MY MOTHER IN THE FACE."
The sounds were nauseating, and, as Dylan felt a wave of sickness passing over him, he decided he would close his eyes before he passed out. He was walking down a hill, and had been steadily doing so since he passed through Hell's entrance. He trusted his feet to feel the grade of the slope and hoped that he

didn't trip, knowing that the outcome would be dire. The further he walked, the quieter it became until the siren seemed to be far in the distance. He decided to open his eyes.

His eyes slowly acclimated and shapes began to form. Expansive rock walls were on either side of him that seemed to initially extend into nothingness, but seemed to collapse smaller and smaller with each step down a rocky and jagged ramp. Protruding from the rock walls, stretching high into the rocky terrain were massive billboards, most of which were completely black but some of which showed advertisements. He passed under a faded green billboard advertising a small claims lawyer named Jimmy Lavino and immediately felt sick again.

A strip of narrow track lighting was perched impossibly high above him, clicking and popping off and on. It reminded him of the lighting at the Outer Shell and he wished he was there. He wanted his body to stop. He wanted to run. He immediately wondered why he ever wanted to get into this place. Another sharp nudge in the back forced him to walk forward. The pathway became increasingly narrow, and the ceiling above them, which once looked to be at an impossible height, seemed to be almost falling on top of them, dropping down the lower they got.

"Single file!" Dylan heard one of the guards shout behind him, as the Walkers ahead of him slowed their step tucking behind one another. Dylan submissively fell in line as the walls on the corridor narrowed to an arm's length. He looked ahead and, amidst the dull light of a dying bulb, he saw a bright green glow. Immediately every horror movie that Dylan had ever seen came flooding into his mind, and he imagined the green to be the glow of eyes belonging to some long dead mythological creature waiting to feast on the flesh of the dead.

Dylan knew it was a demon, an eater of souls. Why he thought he could just walk right into the mouth of Hell and not be immediately eaten by a monster was pure idiocy on his part. He wondered why he had done this to himself before remembering that he had all but given up on his plan to enter Hell and that is when it decided to welcome him in.

Drawing nearer, Dylan calmed down. He heard no growling or gnashing of teeth, just tranquil silence. He realized that he no longer heard the pulsating noise that was so present when he first descended into Hell. He now heard it faint and tame, a long way off in the distance, ebbing quieter with each step towards the newly present green glow.

"Slow!" a guard shouted behind him, as his fellow comrades decreased their pace to a near crawl as Watchers spaced themselves out to the sides of the now single file line. Dylan looked towards the light again and saw what appeared to be the outline of a door, a faint light emitting through the cracks. Although he was walking towards the green glow, it no longer appeared menacing. He realized what they were approaching was indeed a door, and the green glow above it was not the twisted eyes of some horrifying beast but a sign, like the open sign in the window of a convenience store, neon and bright.

"Stop!" A Watcher yelled behind them as the lead Walker stopped just in front of the door practically brushing his nose up against it.

Dylan was still about fifty yards away, but he could see the entrance they were presumably about to walk through was made of metal and had one of those bars across the front that you push open, like the ones you see in high school gymnasiums. The sign that Dylan had first seen in the distance was legible now. It read "Admissions" in glowing green letters.

A Watcher walked to the front of the Line, fumbled with a large set of keys, unlocked the door and pushed it open. A sharp ray of light shot through it. It was an intensely bright and sickening light, like the piercing flash of a camera. Many of the Walkers squinted, as their eyes needed time to adjust to the previous darkness.

"ONE AT A TIME, HAVE YOUR ID NUMBERS READY!"

Dylan watched as the Watcher stepped to the side and began talking to the first Walker in Line. He couldn't make out what they were saying, but it appeared the Watcher was asking him questions, the Walker responding with short answers. The Watcher nodded his head in approval, and the Walker stepped through the door into the light.

The second Walker stepped forward and seemed to answer the same round of questions before stepping through the door herself. There were probably thirty people in front of Dylan, but the number grew smaller as each stepped forward, answered a series of questions and stepped through the door. Dylan didn't know exactly what they were asking, but he was sure he didn't have the right answers. He had heard something about an id number but obviously didn't have one of those. As the number of Walkers before him decreased and he got closer to the front of the Line, he tried to listen in to hear what the Watchers were asking.

"Name and ID number?" was the first question he was able to make out.

"Adam Sheff. 666-125-7845."

"Any contact with..."

"No, sir."

"....counselor....proper paperwork...."

Inhabitant number 666-125-7845 walked through the door and out of Dylan's sight.

The next Walker came forward. Dylan was next in line.

"Name and ID number."

"Zach Collins. 666-453-7654"

"Any contact with the living?"

"No, sir."

"Your surface visit is complete. Please report to counselor Stevenson's office to fill out the proper paperwork." Inhabitant 666-453-7654 stepped into the door.

Dylan was next. He swallowed hard and stepped forward.

"Name and ID number," the guard asked him without looking up from his clipboard.

"Umm, Vince Carter," he said, saying the name of the New Jersey Nets basketball star that he had watched highlights of the night before on television. He didn't know why coming up with a fake name would somehow be better than telling them his own name, as neither one of them would belong there. But he did it anyway. "Number 666-123-6666....6."

 The guard looked up from his clipboard and at Dylan. He drew closer and inhaled a whiff of Dylan's breath.

"What's that smell?" he asked.

"I'm sorry?" Dylan responded.

The Watcher took a step closer to Dylan and sniffed the air around him.

"Is that whiskey?" he asked. "Have you been drinking?"

"Not for awhile," Dylan responded.

The guard dropped his head and rolled his eyes. "Hey Boggins," the guard said. "We got another one."

From behind Dylan, Boggins, a hulking figure of a man, came walking towards Dylan, stopping in front of him and grabbing him by the lapel.

"How did you get in here?" Boggins asked

"Through the front door, like everyone else," Dylan responded.

"Do you know what front door you just wandered into? Do you

have any idea where you are right now? Do you know how much fucking paperwork I'll have to do now?"

"Sorry?" Dylan responded.

"Wear this, genius," Boggins said, pulling Dylan closer and slapping a large vinyl sticker in the shape of the letter 'Z' on his otherwise pristine jumpsuit.

"Take Mr. Zebulon Pike, the great explorer, down to the C ward and put him with the others," Boggins said, shoving Dylan towards the door.

The guard who had asked Dylan the initial round of questions put his arm around Dylan and escorted him through the door where all the other Inhabitants that had gone through were waiting.

"You just made the biggest mistake of your life, my friend," he said before closing the door in Dylan's face. "Welcome to Hell."

Chapter 29

John was drunk, but not nearly as drunk as Chris. Together, the two polished off John's flask, which had contained 22 oz. of Jim Beam Black. For John, it was enough to get him a good solid buzz, which actually helped him think a little clearer than normal. Chris was completely shit faced, which made him think more like how John normally thought, so their goal to sit down and think of a plan to rescue Dylan had gotten a little off track.

"How come in court, no one ever uses the evil twin defense?" Chris asked.

"The evil twin defense?" John answered.

"Yeah, think about it. You tell the jury that you had a long lost twin that, I don't know, escaped from a mental institution when you both were young and no one's been able to find him since. Since then he's been running around committing all sorts of crimes, especially this one in question. That's who the eyeball witness saw, not me but the evil twin."

"Eyeball witness? I'm not sure that's the right term," John said.

"You're getting off the point. What I'm saying is that someone sees ya do something illegal and turns ya in. They think they nail you and you tell them, 'sure, it looked just like me, but it was my twin, he's evil, man.'" Then they say, "well we got DNA evidence," and you say, "well, he's my twin, we're practically the same guy. Bam!"

"You really think that would hold up in court?"

Chris paused and contemplated this for a moment.

"No. But it would make at least one jury member think about it. All you have to do is present reasonable doubt. You get one jury member to slightly buy in and you got yourself a hung jury, eventually they'll drop everything. Boom!"

"How did we start talking about this," John asked.

"You said something about the legal system being color blind, and I reminded you that people of color have a way harder time proving their innocence. Then you said some ignorant shit about 'if the legal system was racist, why did OJ Simpson get off?' and I said there are a lot of ways to get off after you commit a crime: One is money and two...pretend you have a long lost twin...man, I am drunk."

"Well, let's get back to the question at hand. How do we get our boy back?"

"We just go in there, man," Chris slurred. "We just go in with guns blazing. Who's gonna stop us? We go into town, we load the fuck up on weapons and we go in there and start busting some skulls."

"I agree with you in theory because, believe me, it sounds bad ass," John said. "But I feel like they have prepared for that. I just have a feeling the line of defense they have in Hell is pretty legit. Don't they have that big dog, Cerbasomething?"

"Cerbarus? The three-headed Hell dog? I guess I didn't think about that. But fuck all that man, we're really gonna let a dog stop us from barreling into Hell and rescuing our friend?"

"A dog, no, but a three headed Hell-hound, possibly, probably. There are probably a million things down there just as bad if not worse. We need to be tactical. We need to be silent. We need to sneak!" John's pupils got wide and he straightened his posture. "That's it! I know everything there is to know about sneaking. No one will even see us! We'll sneak all the way to the Devil's throne completely undetected. "

"Are you talking about that stupid blog?" Chris asked.

"The blog is not stupid. The blog is a study in human nature. I've followed workers from their office to their car. I've followed mothers and their children home from daycare. One time I followed a police officer and his trained watch dog from the county jail to the doughnut shop."

"And how many times have people caught you?"

"A couple, I guess," John answered. "But those were in the early stages. I've been honing my craft."

"I am probably going to regret saying this, and it's probably just because I've been drinking, but I'm willing to give it a shot. But, John, if you get me killed, I swear to God I will..."

"Best not to think about that right now, my man. Just know that you are following one of the premier sneakers this world has ever seen."

"Air Jordan is a premier sneaker. You, I'm not so sure about."

"Just trust me, Chris."

"OK, I'm going to trust you. What's our plan?"

"First, start gathering up as many small stones as you can. When the line comes back around this way, we're gonna need to create a diversion, then we're gonna walk right in like we own the place."

Chris wasn't sure when the line would next come through. He was only hoping it came quick before he started to rethink this immensely horrible idea.

Chapter 30

Tommy Shareef was standing above a bloody Inhabitant, stroking the once pristine blade of a butcher knife, cleaning off a line of fresh blood. The Inhabitant below him, struggled and gasped, trying to make sense of the vicious assault he had just suffered at the hands of Shareef. Had they been on Earth, the Inhabitant would've likely bled out by now and died. But being already dead, the Inhabitant felt an increasing amount of pain that really had no way of stopping.

Tommy Shareef smiled at the Inhabitant's misery and walked proudly over to Gregory Irons, who had watched in delight as the assault took place.

"Well done, ol' boy, well done," he began. "That's what I call torture. I don't think I've ever heard a person make the noises he was making. You're a very talented man. Did you see that?" Irons said to Daman and Neville Black, who were cowering in the corner.

They too had watched Shareef use a variety of sharp instruments to practically carve up the whimpering Inhabitant, but had not found the same delight in it that Irons had.

"P-p-pretty impressive," Neville stammered back, "a very impressive display of carnage indeed."

"Very messy," Daman said.

"Can I ask why he chose to cut off most of the Inhabitant's fingers? That seemed a bit excessive," Neville said.

"Very excessive," Daman said.

"Excessive? Look at him," Irons said motioning to the whimpering Inhabitant. "He is completely broken thanks to ol' Tommy here.

He will never be the same again. The things that happened to him today will haunt him forever. This is the worst thing that has ever happened to him, and it will happen again and again." The Inhabitant let out a dull whimper and covered his head with his awkwardly disfigured hands.

"Why would we do it again?" Daman asked. "That poor man is very scared."

"You're worried about him?" Irons asked walking towards Daman and Neville. The two took a cautious step backwards. "You worry about the dregs of the Earth, the very people you are sworn to make repent? These people are not your friends. These people are your slaves. Just who the fuck do you think you are?"

Daman swallowed hard, cowering in the corner that Irons had backed them into.

"I'm the Devil, right?"

"Not anymore you're not. The weak may inherit the Earth, but the strong will take over the underworld. I was gonna wait for the right time to tiddly wink you, but I can't sit around no more! Tommy, put them in a cell!"

"What?" Neville shouted. "You can't be serious!"

Tommy Shareef, bloody blade in hand, descended on them. Daman and Neville, having nowhere else to go, slowly crouched down and recoiled in fear at the approaching mad man. Neville Black peed a little in his trousers.

"You pawns! I can't afford you two bumbling idiots interfering anymore. From now on, you two are Inhabitants of Hell just like the rest of them, and, if you think I was excessive before, just wait until I unleash my fury upon you! Everyone will rue the day that they mocked Steven Arber, I mean the Dragon!"

With a snap of his fingers, four other guards rushed out of the shadows and, along with Tommy Shareef, grabbed Daman and

Neville, and violently shoved them into the caverns of the underworld.

Gregory Irons could not stop laughing. His blood-shot eyes darted back and forth with excitement and a tingling feeling rushed throughout his limbs. He had done it. Hell was now his.

Chapter 31

The door that they thrust Dylan through led to an elevator. The elevator, massive and mechanical, was of the freight variety. It creaked and rattled, carrying its cargo slowly but surely down into the depths of the underworld.

Nobody spoke and, save for the mechanical hum of the turning of the elevator gears, it was quiet. It was a quiet Dylan had never experienced before. It was unencumbered by the usual murmur of a heartbeat or the expulsion of breath. He was in a tiny, moving room full of corpses and his rapidly beating heart was the only one making noise.

Dylan tried to talk his slowly sobering brain out of going into complete panic mode. This is where he wanted to be the whole time, right? He had succeeded! For the first time in his life, he had set out to do something and accomplished it.

But why? Why was this his ultimate goal? Was this the great master plan? Was it really to help a girl that he barely knew? What kind of moron would go through with this? What kind of self-loathing, idiotic, lame-brained total asshole son of a....Dylan caught himself again and focused on breathing slow and deliberate, trying not to panic and deal with whatever happened as it came. The elevator stopped and the door opened.

"Booking! 88A!" a guard in the middle of the pack cried out. When the door opened, the bodies all around him began shuffling towards the open door, waiting for their time to exit. When there was space available, Dylan took a step forward in an attempt to do the same. Half a step forward and he felt a tugging on his collar pulling him backwards.

"Not you," Boggins said as he yanked back on Dylan's shirt. "You stay here."

Dylan fell back towards Boggins, sidling up alongside him like an untrained puppy on a leash. The elevator emptied as Dylan peered through a break in the crowd and saw what appeared to be an office setting not far off in the distance, track lighting and partition walls. Although this whole experience was brutally strange, Dylan couldn't help but wonder why such a setup would exist in the underworld. Where was all the fire and brimstone?

More and more people exited the elevator until only Dylan, Boggins and one other person remained. Boggins gave a thumbs up to the guard standing by the elevator door, who hit a switch before exiting. The door closed and the elevator began to descend back down.

"Just the three of us, huh?" Dylan said to Boggins.

"Yep," Boggins tersely answered.

"Where are we going?"

"Down."

Seeing that he was not going to get much information from his captor, Dylan looked over across the elevator to his other travel companion.

The man was sweating profusely and breathing nervously. Dylan noticed the man, unlike him and everyone else in Line, was not wearing an orange suit but jeans and a blue sweater. Still, though, a large Z was affixed to his chest. There was something else about this man that Dylan did not notice at first, but was very aware of now. He watched the stranger's chest expand and collapse with each short breath and realized that this man, like him, was still alive. The elevator descended down into the belly of Hell for what seemed like forever. The three men rode in silence the rest of the way after their initial conversation. The only sound was the slow hum of the elevator cable, creaking and stretching against the rusted gears.

Dylan wanted to start up a conversation again and maybe get some dialogue out of his living companion. Every time he opened his mouth to speak, though, he looked over at the guard who appeared to have violent intent in his eyes, like he was hoping Dylan would say something so he could physically make him stop talking. After what Dylan estimated to be about 20 minutes, the elevator came to a stop and Dylan felt a dull thud under his feet. They had taken the elevator to its literal last stop, hitting the ground floor.

"Is this us?" Dylan said to the guard watching the iron door creep slowly open.

"Yes," he responded. "Get out."

Dylan and the other man cautiously stepped forward and peeked out. Outside of the door was a narrow hallway, barely lit by a series of sickly blue lights with wire grates on them. Every few feet, carved into the rock, was a metal door with a small window just wide enough to look through in the upper left-hand corners of each door.

"Walk!" The impatient guard said, shoving Dylan in the back. Dylan forcefully moved forward as his living companion sidled up beside him.

Although Dylan did not know this person at all, he trusted him, as he represented the only thing that appeared to be normal in an otherwise bizarre situation. As they walked, Dylan tried to look into the windows to see if he could see what was inside. Although very narrow, they were wide enough to see inside, but Dylan saw only darkness through the glass. He wondered what was in the rooms and which one was meant for him.

He tried not to think what would be waiting for them on the other side of the doors, but he hoped that maybe it would be something that would bring them a quick and painless death so that this whole ordeal would be over. On and on they walked past door after door until the hallway ahead of them was ending, hitting a rock wall and intersecting with another hallway, running in the opposite direction. When they reached the intersection, the guard demanded they stop.

The two men obeyed and the guard walked in front of them towards the last door of the hallway on their right. The guard slid a smaller compartment in the door open, produced a set of keys, unlocked three locks down the left side of the door and muscled the door open. The guard turned back around to face his prisoners and motioned into the cell like a carnival worker offering up a Ferris wheel to a young couple.

"In ya go," he said.

Cautiously, Dylan and the other prisoner peered into the room. While it was dark, Dylan could see that the room was large. He squinted to see the back wall and saw shadows moving back and forth through the thick and silent blackness. He didn't know what they were, but he thought he heard them whisper.

"I said in!" the guard shouted, shoving them forward onto the floor of the cell. They hit the ground on top of each other in a tangled mess.

"Nighty night," the guard said as he exited the room and coldly shut the door behind him.

"Wait!" Dylan shouted.

He struggled to his feet just in time to reach the door as it closed with a loud mechanical clang. The sound of several locks retightening themselves was heard before it was deathly quiet again. He turned back around to see his companion, who was now on his feet, dusting himself off. For the first time since they had seen each other, Dylan opened his mouth to say something to him but was immediately met with a "shhhh" by the man. Dylan froze as the man kept his finger up towards Dylan.

From the dark, the shadows Dylan had seen when he first looked into the cell were now closer to them. All around them shadows dropped out of the walls, sneaking through the cracks of the foundation. The two men backed towards the cell door. The shadows continued to awkwardly move towards them.

"This is it," Dylan said as he waited for the shadows to descend upon him.

Chapter 32

John and Chris had completely passed out. The combination of alcohol, the initial rush of excitement and the boredom of waiting for the Line to return had reduced the pair into motionless, snoring, whisky-soaked piles of incapacitation. John's head was resting squarely on Chris' stomach. As they drooled and snored in peaceful slumber, the Line marched towards them and the usual cadence of feet grew louder. Chris woke up first and heard the sound. He shot up quickly, knocking John's head off of him and onto the ground.

"John, wake up, man. Wake up, they're here!"

"Who is?" John asked through half open eyes.

"Them! Them, man, the Line! We gotta get up, man. Where are those rocks we gathered?"

"What do we need rocks for?"

"You son of a...you said we needed them for a diversion. We spent 20 minutes searching for the perfect ones, remember?"

"Ah yeah, totally, the diversion. Yeah, I guess we can throw them or something. That might work."

"That might work? You told me you were the premier sneaker of our time. You said you had a plan!"

"That's the thing about the art of sneaking. It's an improvisational art form. Things change as you go. It's like jazz."

"I don't have time to sit here and argue with you right now, just get up before they see us."

Chris grabbed John by his arm and lifted him off the ground only to drag him a few yards and then shove him back down again behind a bush.

"OK," Chris began. "Maybe this diversion thing isn't such a bad idea. Once the door opens we'll chuck some of the bigger ones in our opposite direction, hope that some of the Watchers go over to investigate and then we'll sneak into this bitch. Easy, right?"

"Easy, man. They'll never see us. We're fucking invisible."

"OK, here they come. Get down. Once the door is all the way open, it's show time."

As the line approached, John and Chris crouched down behind a bush about 100 yards away from the nearest walker. Without speaking, Chris nodded at John, trying to signal him that he should throw his first rock.

"What?" John mouthed shrugging his shoulders.

Chris made a miming gesture of throwing a rock, pointing at John and then pointing where he wanted him to throw it.

John shook his head in complete bewilderment.

"Throw a fucking rock already!" Chris demanded in a whispered yell.

"Oh, yeah. Good idea." With no attempt to hide his location, John stood up from his hiding place and threw a rock, not away from the Line like they had discussed, but right at the Line.

"What the fuck?" Chris said before he realized he was too late, as a baseball size rock was now headed straight towards an unsuspecting Walker. It connected with a loud "thwap," striking the back of one of the orange clad jumpsuit wearers, knocking him forward as he collided with the Walker in front of him.

Chris, horrified by his friend's stupidity, yanked him hard towards the ground and back down behind the bush.

"Are you fucking kidding me?" he asked John.

"What?"

"You just hit someone with that rock! That is not what we talked about before, you were supposed to throw it away from them to create a diversion."

"Yeah I knew that was the plan but then you started using all of these crazy hand signals and whispering and I got confused. "

"God damn it, you little shit. This is the last time I let you get me into trouble. I swear to...." before Chris could finish, he was distracted by a pair of shadows now hanging over them. They belonged to a pair of very scary looking, angry Watchers.

"Get up," one of them said. Not wanting to upset the weapon-wielding Hell dwellers any further, the two complied.

"It was him," Chris said pointing to John.

"Whoa. Really, dude? You're just gonna sell me out like that after all we've been through? I thought we were tight."

"Shut up," said the other, larger Watcher. "What exactly do you think you're doing here?" He asked.

"Creating a diversion," John said.

"John!" Chris yelled. "He said shut up! Listen to the man, and let me speak! We're not doing anything, just out for a stroll in the woods. My friend here thought he saw a pond and tried to skip a stone over it. We're really sorry."

"You are attempting to interfere with an Inhabitant herding. This is your one official warning. The next infraction will be dealt with extreme prejudice."

Chris glanced behind the guard and saw that the entrance to Hell was slowly opening. He knew that this was their only chance but couldn't think of a way to get by the Watchers. He remembered what had happened to Dylan the day that he had been caught in the Line and just didn't think he felt like taking a beating today.

"Absolutely, sir," he began. "I completely understand, this whole thing is just a big misunderstanding, and we will absolutely leave you alone from here on out."

"Please see that you do," the Watcher responded. "Please understand that future interferences will be..."

"It wasn't us," John abruptly said.

"Excuse me?" the Watcher responded.

"It wasn't me. It was my evil twin. He threw the rock and ran off into the woods, that way. If you start now, you can probably catch him. Go on," John made a dismissive motion towards the guard.

"Not now, John," Chris said through clenched teeth.

"Trust me," he whispered back loud enough that the Watchers could clearly hear him. "Go on, right over there. I think I see him. Look."

Although not buying it for a second, the two Watchers glanced over their shoulder in the direction of John's fake, evil twin. John grabbed Chris by the shoulder and jerked him away from the Watchers. "Run!" he shouted.

Before Chris could protest, he was being dragged away from the Watchers in the direction of Hell's open entrance. "Go, go, go!" John yelled. "Don't stop, they're right behind us!"

Back on the hill, neither Watcher moved.

"How many of these fucking people do we have to put up with in a day?" One guard asked the other. "I feel like this is all we do now."

"Let him go. The Dragon said he wants as many people down there as he possibly can get. He said he's building an army."

"Oh yeah, that's right. I mean how insulting can you be? Like, hello, what exactly does he think people like us do?"

"Don't even get me started on that guy. I honestly think we were better off when the Devil ran things. Let those two go for now. I honestly don't feel like filling out the paperwork right now anyway. Damn Dragon is running us ragged."

Unaware of the conversation going on behind them, Chris and John ran past the Line of Inhabitants and into Hell's open mouth. They had no idea what they were doing or where they were going but so far, everything was going perfectly to plan.

In the silence, John and Chris both noticed just how loud the other one was breathing. Crouched behind two separate rocks, they shot daggers at one another attempting to convey that the other was giving their location away as the pair gasped to catch their breaths. After they sprinted through Hell's entrance, they found themselves on Hell's front porch, the very same spot that Dylan had found himself only hours before. Unlike Dylan, though, Chris and John were able to frantically explore the vast opening much more than their friend, who had been forcibly escorted by much less apathetic guards.

With John leading the way, the two men sprinted down the first tunnel they saw, which was only dimly lit by torches, until they were sure that no one was following them. In actuality, of course, they had not been followed at all. The Dragon needed numbers for his army, and the once airtight security team had lowered their guard. Soon, they would start luring people from Earth on purpose. John and Chris were miles away from the closest guard, but were still convinced that the other one was going to get them caught. "Shut up," Chris mouthed to John, incensed at his partners near asthmatic wheezing.

"Fuck you," he mouthed back, convinced it was Chris's breathing that was the real problem.

Chris glared at John and shook his head, dragging his finger across his neck in the universal symbol for "I'm going to kill you."

John gestured back at Chris, shoving an imaginary phallus in his mouth and rolling his tongue in conjunction with the movement, the international symbol for "suck my dick."

"What is that?" Chris asked. He heard something nearby, perhaps a voice.

John shook his head and stopped shifting for long enough for them both to listen. At first it was silent, but then Chris heard it again. It was the sound of a muffled voice, a woman's voice, but Chris could not make out what she was saying.

Chris motioned to John for him to slowly rise and check out the source of the voice. It appeared to be close by. John shook his head and pointed to Chris, suggesting that he should be the one to check out the noise.

"Same time," Chris whispered. He held up three fingers to John and counted them down slowly to one. When Chris made a fist for zero, they both shot out from their hiding places and darted their heads around trying to discover the source of the voice. No one was around them. The voice appeared to be coming over the other side of a steep drop off fifteen feet in front of them. The two crept towards the ledge and looked over. On the other side were thousands, upon thousands of discarded fax machines, copiers and printers. The fax machine closest to them, a Brother Intellifax 4100-e, was speaking to them. "This long distance call requires you to dial ten digits, please hang up and try again. This long distance call requires you to dial ten digits, please hang up and try again. This long distance call requires you to dial ten digits, please hang up and try again."

As if sensing their presence, the other machines started up, all displaying some sort of error message. Some were vocal about it, others just made sick, coughing noises as they struggled to complete the task they were designed for. The sound was maddening.

"If you need help, hang up and dial 411. If you'd like to make a call please hang up. Receiver 404 error error error. Paper jam paper jam whirrrrrrrrrrrrr"

"What is this?" John asked.

"I don't know, but this is freaking me out," Chris said. "We have to keep moving. This is sure to give us away."

Chris stepped away from the office-machine graveyard and peered into the impossibly long passage way. He grabbed John and led him in the opposite direction from which they came, trying to collect his thoughts and get away from the maddening clicks, whirs and prerecorded messages that still incessantly called out to them.

One hundred feet in the opposite direction and the noise had quieted down. Regaining his senses, Chris picked up the faint smell of mildew in the air. Water was close by. He bent over and touched the rocky floor, it was damp. He turned back to John, and raised his hands halfway up his body in a gesture of acquiescence. As much as he derived pleasure from arguing with John, he knew that, if they were going to get through this, they had to do it together.

"Look," he began. "I'm sorry about earlier. This is obviously a stressful situation, and I think I'm taking it out on you."

"I agree. You've been a real dick," John said.

"I think we need to head down this tunnel, because I think there is a water source at some point. I don't know where it's coming from, but I can almost feel it in the air. Can you feel it too?"

"I guess so," John said. "But why is that a good thing?"

"Maybe it leads to an exit. These tunnels may go on forever, and then we'll get lost and never find Dylan. I say we go towards water. You with me?"

"You know it!" John enthusiastically said, slapping Chris's hand causing a loud smack that echoed throughout the length of the tunnel.

"OK good, but we gotta be quiet. The art of sneaking, man. Let's do this."

The two stood side by side, staring into the vast cavern and hoping they would make it out of the other side alive.

"Well, we're off to see the Wizard," Chris said.

"You said it, man. Fucking Gandalf."

Chapter 33

Dylan had learned the fight-or-flight theory in high school and was wondering why no one ever discussed the third option: freezing. Currently, Dylan was in the midst of the third option as he watched dozens of shadows descend upon him. He decided he was not going to move at all. Fuck it. He was going to let whatever was going to happen to him happen. He had gotten himself into this mess and he was too tired to fight.

He looked over at his living companion and saw that he too was choosing the same option, only looking less resolved about it as tiny beads of sweat trickled down his brow. Dylan closed his eyes and waited for an unknown, but inevitable amount of pain. Then, with his eyes clenched tight, one of the shadows spoke.

"Pigs!" It shouted. "Those fucking pigs. Always picking on everyone. Are you guys OK?"

"You mean us? Are you asking if we're OK?" Dylan asked.

"Yeah," the shadow said moving even closer. "Those guards think they're such tough guys. Always tossing people around. Fucking rent a cops. You sure you're OK?"

"Yeah, I think so. Just a few scratches. I'm sorry, but I still can't see you very well."

"Close your eyes for a little bit more. It'll help you adjust to the darkness."

Dylan took the advice and pressed the palms of his hands up against his eye lids. Opening his eyes again, he squinted at the man who was talking to him. He could see him more clearly now.

He looked to be about Dylan's age with a spotty red beard, shoulder length hair tied into a ponytail and a blue bandana tied around his forehead.

"What's your name?" the shadow asked.

"Vince Cart..."Dylan started before realizing he didn't have to keep his former lie intact about being the small forward for the Nets. "Dylan."

"Nice to meet you, Dylan. I'm Brian. What about your friend? What's his name?"

Dylan looked over at the man he had ridden down in the elevator with and realized that neither one of them had said a word to one another since they started on their journey.

"Ya know, I'm not even sure. We haven't officially been introduced yet. What's your name, pal?"

The man, looked nervously at Dylan and then back at the man in the bandana. He squinted a few times in his own attempt to adjust his eyes to the darkness, but said nothing.

"Not a big talker, huh?"

The man opened his mouth like he was about to say something but closed it again smiling faintly at Dylan.

"Do you speak English?" Brian asked.

"English?" The man finally replied as if it was the first word he had heard said that he recognized but then replied with a solemn, "No."

"Spanish, Espanol?"

"No."

"French?" Brian asked.

"Oui," the man replied "Je suis Francais Je ne parle pas anglais," he said.

"Oh that's rad!" Brian said. "Don't worry, I think the goth guy speaks some French. We'll introduce you to him later."

Dylan looked to the back of the room and guessed that it went back a couple hundred yards. It appeared to be full of people and, while no one other than Brian was speaking to him directly, he could hear them whispering to one another. It was like *The Wizard of Oz* where Dorothy first lands in Oz and the Munchkins are gossiping. He couldn't wait for the Wicked Witch of the West to show up. All of them, Brian included, had 'Zs' on their clothing.

"What are you guys?" Dylan asked Brian.

"I suppose we're just like you man," Brian said. "People who wandered through the big gate into Hell. Some of us did it on purpose, but some of us just sort of woke up here. Either way, once they find out what we are, they slap these stickers on us, give us a suit and throw us in this room. I see you already got the suit part figured out. How'd you get down here?"

"I'm not sure how I got here. I was in the woods and then the next thing I knew I was walking through the door. Is that what happened to you?"

"I guess you could call it that," Brian said. "Truth be told, I'm not sure if I remember the last part of it either. I had been laid off from my job and was sitting in the woods with a .22 hunting rifle, contemplating ending it all. Then I heard a weird sound coming from far off, people marching. I saw everyone coming towards me, a few people that you see in this very room, and then I think I sorta blacked out. The next thing I know I was being yelled at and shoved into the elevator that brought me down here. Pretty much everyone in this room has a similar story. None of us died, but we all ended up here anyway. This room is their way of separating us from the rest of them before they figure out what they're gonna do with us. That's why they slap these letters on us. We still don't exactly know what they stand for. Regardless of whether we meant to end up here or not, they appear intent on keeping us."

"What are they gonna do with us?" Dylan asked?

"We're not really sure," Brian said. "Every couple of days one of those fascist guards will come down here and haul one of us out of here. Sometimes, they come right back and the people who do say they just get questioned by someone in an office. Some don't come back at all. I've been here a week and they've taken a few of us. There's no way of knowing who's next. What about you, man. What brought you down here?"

  He hesitated, not knowing how far he should go and if he should tell them about Lauren and how this was his plan all along. Without really thinking about it Dylan blurted out, "My mom died."

Brian looked at him with genuine concern and the throng of shadow people let out a hushed and sympathetic sigh.

"My mom killed herself," Dylan continued more for his own recollection. This was the first time he really had time to think about it. "We'd been trying for a few weeks...my friends and I. Then I walked out of my job, I got drunk, my mom died and now I'm here. I'm not supposed to be here."

Brian walked over to him and put a sympathetic hand on his shoulder. "I thought that at first too. All of us did. But all of us have come to terms with the fact that we were fed up with our lives and, somehow, this place called out to us. It was ready for us. Every single one of us looked at this as escape. We all succeeded. For better or worse, we succeeded. Life can't disappoint us anymore. As fucked up as it sounds, we're home."

"So let me get this straight. Every single person in here just walked right in? Everyone in here is still alive?"

"Well, almost everyone," Brian said. "That goth guy and his little buddy claimed they've been down here the whole time. Hey, that reminds me, we should call him up here and see if he can make any sense out of ol' Pierre here," Brian said motioning to the Frenchman. "That guy claims he can speak every language there is. Hey Dorrian!" Brian called out into the shadows, "Can you come on up here and work your supposed multi-linguist tongue?"

"Why you say sahposed?" came a voice from the back of the room. Emerging from the shadows was an awkward little man in a tweed suit and slicked-back hair, sidled up beside a man that looked a little like Alice Cooper with a bad goatee. A black cape hung around his shoulders.

"Well it's just you've been saying for days now that you speak every language there is, and now's the time to put it to the test, that's all."

"First off," the little man in the tweed coat said. "His name is actually Daman, though he would prefer you to refer to him as the Dark One or His Lordship, something along those lines. Second of all, he is excellent in all forms of verbal communication, with the exception of Icelandic and European and Latin American forms of Spanish."

"It's dee tenses. Very confuse." Daman said.

"Dylan, these are the ones I was telling you about, the ones who claim they have been here long before any of us, but for some reason were sentenced to this room by a big lizard or something. Buncha hooey if you ask me."

"The Dragon," Neville Black corrected. "And I'd be careful what you say about him. He's always listening."

"Right. Well, gents, this is Dylan and this gentleman over here speaks French, and we would love it if you could use that remarkable ability of yours to make him feel right at home."

"It ees granted," Daman said.

Daman knelt down next to the Frenchman and began a whispered conversation.

Dylan watched the three men, having no idea that one of these men, just hours ago, was the leader of the underworld and how sometime in the near future, this same man would help him in his attempt to escape it.

"Dat man, Acel. He said he come here because of da pain," Daman said to Dylan and Brian. "Da pain was just too much."

Daman had talked to Acel for about five minutes in the corner of the dark cell finding out information that he could relay back to the others about why and how he had ended up there.

Mr. Black had retreated back to the shadows and had fallen asleep, using his tweed blazer for a pillow. This made the task of deciphering the Devil's jibberish extremely difficult.

"What pain?" Dylan asked. "What sort of pain was he in?"

"Acel said da pain come after da hope die," Daman cryptically continued. "He come from France to make da pies and he make them good. Then, da fire come and burn it all down, and so went all of his money. So he followed the Travelers into my domain."

Dylan stared hard at Daman for a moment, realizing he shockingly understood some of what had just been said. He couldn't tell to what level some of these phrases were being lost in translation – from the man who spoke no English or from the man who spoke his own brand of English.

"So," he said, "he came from France to make pies? He was a baker?"

"Yes, baker. He said he bake in the sky, but then the fire burn the sky."

"The fire burned the sky?" Dylan asked.

"Wait," said a man's voice from the shadows. Emerging from them was a small man in a tattered orange jumpsuit. He had brown hair, a crooked nose and small wire-framed glasses.

Sorry to interrupt, but I overheard what you were talking about. I think I know what he means."

"Which part?" Dylan asked

"The oven-in-the-sky part. That bakery on Carpenter Ave., the one that just burned down, was named Four Dans Ciel or something like that. Someone told me it translated to the Oven in the Sky. That must be what he meant."

Dylan looked over at Daman for affirmation. "Well, is it?"

"Yes, da oven in sky. He lost everything in da flames. Now he come to my domain to live amongst...." Daman paused for dramatic effect. "...the dead."

"Any idea what any of that means?" Dylan asked the man with the glasses.

"This joker's been saying stuff like that ever since he came down with that squirrely dude with the suit. He thinks he's the Devil."

"How dare you challenge me? I am da one Dark Lord and will vanquish all who oppose me" Daman said to the men. Dylan noticed that the comical way the man was speaking wasn't as noticeable. The man suddenly appeared more menacing, more sinister.

"Dark Lord, ha!" the man with the glasses scoffed as he turned and walked away. "Are you the Devil or Darth Vader?"

For the first time in a while, Dylan laughed as well. This whole situation was ridiculous, and Daman was just too much for him to take right now. He let out a hearty chuckle that immediately caught the attention of Daman.

"Why do you laugh?" Daman asked him.

"I'm sorry man, it's not you. This whole thing is just insane. Haaha. I mean, what a day, huh? That whole Devil thing is just too much for me right now. "

Dylan looked back over at Daman and saw that, while he was not responding to Dylan, his lips were moving. He was chanting something.

"Rakta, rudhira, loha, ha. Rakta, rudhira, loha, ha. Rakta, rudhira, loha, ha. Rakta, rudhira, loha, ha." Daman repeated over and over again.

"What are you saying?" Dylan asked. Daman did not hear him and repeated the mantra. "Rakta, rudhira, loha, ha. Rakta, rudhira, loha, ha. Rakta, rudhira, loha, ha."

Dylan lowered his head and looked into Daman's eyes. His once-green irises were glowing a dull, fire red and Dylan took a sharp step back. "What the fuck?" he said.

Dylan's legs began to quiver. It was coupled with a strange tingling sensation like his legs were falling asleep, but he felt a strange compulsion to move them in a direction he was sure his brain was not aware of.

He smelled blood in the air and could feel it building up inside of his nose, ready to spill out in gallons onto the rocky floor. While he was no stranger to nose bleeds, this was different. He felt his body trying to escape through his nostrils. Dylan looked again at Daman, who was still chanting but was now making direct eye contact with him. "What are you doing?" he asked.

Just when Dylan thought his insides were ready to explode, the door to the cell quickly swung open, shooting a dull strand of light into the room. The bursting sensation in Dylan stopped and Daman dropped to the floor like a puppet that had its strings cut.

Through the open door walked two guards. One of them looked around the room and poked a meaty hand towards Dylan. "He's the one," the guard said to the other. "Grab him."

The guard wasted no time in walking towards Dylan, grabbing him and marching him towards the still-open cell door. Daman was on his hands and knees, his face obscured by his stringy hair, panting like he had just run a marathon.

"What were you doing?" Dylan asked him, still being shoved towards the door. "Hey, answer me! What did you do?! What are you!?" Daman never answered, and Dylan was shoved out the door, which slammed behind him with a metal thud.

Silence and darkness returned to the cell as Daman remained on his knees panting and sweating. The other people in the cell had no idea just how close they had come to witnessing the magnificent wrath of the Devil himself.

Chapter 34

John and Chris had been following the water source for about a mile now. The trip took longer than it should, as the two stopped to hide every few hundred steps. Strange noises could be heard coming from the entrance of the tunnel, echoing loudly down the rocky corridor. Each time they did this, the paranoia faded, and they continued to convince themselves that nothing was after them.

Despite being deep inside the underworld, the two walked without needing a flashlight. The corridors were lit up by hundreds of neon signs, most of which were advertising some kind of beer. "Hey, I have that one," John said as they passed a sign with Coors spelled out in familiar cursive.

The trickle of water that they initially followed now turned into a stream, flowing rapidly down a worn-down channel. They were convinced they were close to the tunnel's exit, as the sound of rushing water drew closer.

"What's with all the advertising?" John asked.

"Beats me," Chris said. "I'm guessing they have to cover all their bases."

"What do you mean by that?"

"Well, there must be just as many people down here as there are on Earth, and each of them is different. I think this whole place is set up to make sure that there's a way to torture everyone, literally your own personal Hell."

"Do you think that explains the water? Like for hydrophobes?" John asked. "You sure we should follow it. What if it's not safe?"

"I don't think anything down here can be considered safe," Chris answered. "But the further we walk this way, the further away we get from the guards and the other people who were chasing us. Besides, it might lead to a way out."

"A way out?" John said. "We're trying to get out already? What the hell, man? I thought we were coming down here with guns blazing? Weren't those your words exactly? Yippe kai aye mother fucker. Right? Have you forgotten that we're here to get our friend out?"

Chris stopped walking as well and turned to face John. "What I said before was absolutely out of character. I think you forget how much we had been drinking before we came in here. Now that I've sobered a bit, I'm thinking our best plan of action may be to find the easiest way out, avoid being killed and start from scratch with a new plan. You understand?"

John contemplated this for a second before saying, "Fuck that. I say we keep walking this way until we figure out a way to find Dylan."

"Yeah, that's what I'm saying, except I think we keep walking the same way because I think there might be a way out."

"Well," John began. "At least we both agree that we keep walking this way, right?"

"Yes, I guess we finally agree on something," Chris said and started walking again.

As they continued, the stream turned into a small river, which rushed and white capped ever so slightly. John happily walked behind Chris, who was beginning to get nervous, sensing the end of the tunnel was near and dreading what was on the other side. As the water level continued to rise, he heard John shout, "Look, I can see it. Right up ahead, I think that's the end."

Chris looked off into the distance about 100 yards or so and saw what indeed looked like the mouth of the tunnel.

At its mouth, water flowed over like a blanket, hitting the ground and forming the river they had been following.

"You think we can walk right through it?" John asked, referring to the cascading water.

"Only one way to find out," Chris said. "Let me know how it goes.

"Pussy," John said before dead sprinting away from Chris and towards the mouth of the cave.

"John, wait!" Chris yelled, but John did not answer. He quickened his pace towards the waterfall with no regard to what was on the other side. Chris watched him disappear into the falls.

Chris called out his name but did not get a response. He took a cautious step forward before jumping back, as John ran back through the waterfall.

"Dude, you have to come see this. It's incredible! I'll meet you on the other side!" He said before darting back into the water.

For the first time since they had entered Hell, Chris felt a sense of relief and ran as fast as he could after John, wondering what had gotten him so excited. Chris ran through the waterfall and braced himself to be attacked by something, but on the other side of the waterfall, he was met with only silence. He kept his eyes closed while wiping water off his face before opening them and looking around for John.

What he saw in front of him was absolutely mystifying. He was on the shore of a large pond that was fed by the waterfall they had just run through. On the pond, floating aimlessly, were hundreds of rowboats. Each one contained one person, and all of them were fishing. John was standing at the shore of the pond, staring at the boats in astonishment.

Chris walked over to him and asked, "What the fuck?"

"I know, right?" John said. "I did not expect to see this. There's fish down here?"

"I really don't know. I can't imagine there would be."

"I'm gonna ask. Excuse me!" he shouted to the boaters. "Can I ask you what you're fishing for?"

In unison, every fisherman on the pond looked over and gave John a loud "shhhhhhh." The sound echoed through the cavern.

"Geeze, tough crowd," John said.

One of the boaters started paddling quickly towards them. The two took a step back, not knowing his intentions.

"Hey, you two dummies," he whispered.

Chris and John looked behind them. "Us?" Chris asked.

"No, the other two dummies making all the noise. You're scaring the fish. Keep it down. Come over here."

John and Chris stepped cautiously towards the man. The man was in his 60s and was dressed like a typical fisherman with his vest, waders and hat, but all over an orange jumpsuit. As Chris walked closer, he saw that all the other fishermen were dressed pretty much the same.

"What are you guys doing over here?" the man asked.

"We're not really sure," Chris replied. "We followed the waterfall and we ended up here. We're looking for our friend."

"Is he dead?" the man asked.

"I guess by now he could be," Chris said, "but he wasn't when he arrived."

"Ah, I get it. You're some of those people, the infiltrators. What do they call ya, parasites?"

"Parasites?" Chris asked.

"Well that's what you are, aren't ya? Coming in and trying to poison the environment. We get more of you dummies by the day. I'll never understand it. Your friend the same as you?"

"Yeah, came down earlier though. We kind of lost track of him," Chris said.

"Well, chances are they have him in the cells on the north east corridor. It's a straight shot over the pond."

"What is this?"

"Styx Pond, the ol' fishing hole. I've been coming here for years...every day actually, for 50 years."

"There are fish in here?"

"Oh yeah," the man said. "Well, there are supposed to be. None of us here have actually ever caught anything. It's really frustrating."

"They let you do this, though?" Chris asked.

"More like force us. This is part of our punishment. When I was alive, I fished all of the time and nothing ticked me off more than going out on the lake and getting skunked. For the last 50 years I've been coming here and trying to catch the big one. They tell us if we ever catch one that we will be set free, but, like I said, nothing so far."

"Wow, that's messed up," Chris said.

"Yeah, sure is," the man said. "Anyway, about your friend. Hop in and I'll take you across. Otherwise it's caverns and tunnels for miles and miles. Chances are you'll get lost and die down here. Come on, hop in."

Contemplating a slow painful death by starvation, the two climbed carefully in the tiny rowboat.

"All aboard?" The man joked. "Please sit still and remain as quiet as possible."

The man took his oars and shoved the boat away from the shore. He started paddling, and the three men were soon bobbing rhythmically across the pitch-black waters.

"So, what's the plan once we find him?" John asked in his normal volume.

Before Chris could answer, all of the boats surrounding them again shushed them, and the man in the boat stared at them sternly.

"Total silence," he whispered. "You're scaring the fish."

"I'm sorry, I just really don't think there's fish down here. They're fucking with you."

"Shhhhh!"

"Seems a little ridiculous," John scoffed. "I mean, can't you all figure out there's no fish in here for fucks sake."

"Watch what you say, young man," the fisherman said, "and, for the last time, shut up."

John listened to the man and, for a while, the three men floated along in total silence. The pond seemed to go on forever. It was as deep and dark as the night sky. Reflective and calm, it shot back the image of the three men in the boat. John stared at his reflection listlessly from the wooden vessel. He looked into the eyes of his watery visage and saw something silver flash before causing a ripple through the water. It was a fish.

"I see one!" he yelled out.

"Shuuush," the crowd of boaters responded.

"Seriously, I see a fish! Right over here!"

Hundreds of boaters, frustrated by years of getting skunked and with the promise of a Hell pardon, slammed their oars into the water and started paddling madly towards the boat.

"Uh oh," John said.

The man paddling their boat changed his demeanor suddenly too, grabbing his fishing pole and casting it into the water. "Stay back!" he yelled. "It's mine!"

The boat began to rock and, as the other boats approached in droves, the tiny boat tipped from one side to the other as the fishermen fought for position, throwing elbows and swinging their paddles like axes. Dozens more approached as John and Chris dodged and ducked limbs, oars and fishing line. Chris ducked as a large black oar came flying towards his face. The oar instead struck John right over his head and he fell out of the boat and into the pond.

"John!" Chris yelled, as he tried to grab his friend. As he leaned half out of the boat, another man yanked him by the shirt and sent him flailing into the water as well. The boats continued to paddle towards them, rowing on top of the two as they struggled for air. There was no room to ascend; they were blocked by a ceiling of tiny, wooden boats. They scrambled and swam frantically, looking for a break in the boats, but, every time they saw one, the mass would shift and the gap became too small to swim through.

Totally submerged, they had no way out as hundreds of more boats were on their way over, rapidly constructing their underwater coffin. Chris and John were drowning. The fight was moving out of them and they were getting drowsy. One last push for the surface and the water filling both of their lungs became too much. Chris opened his eyes one last time and looked at John through the murky water. He gave Chris an accepting smile and, as he shrugged, he closed his eyes and died. Chris followed suit seconds later.

The two lifeless bodies lay floating in the water as the fisherman melee continued above them. Both bodies then voided their bowels.

Chapter 35

David Estern was going to die. After Lawrence Thompson's skewed testimony that Estern was completely sane and therefore fit to be executed, the wheels were once again put into motion and the date was set. He now sat in a death chamber waiting for his inevitable fate.

He asked that no member of the Prisoners Helping People program be allowed anywhere near him. He was tired of their religious rhetoric and attempts to save his soul. Knowing what he now knew, he did not see the point. His only final request was to speak with Lawrence Thompson one last time. He had some things he needed to tell him.

He hadn't sat down in hours and paced nervously in his cell. Growing up, the uncertainty of what would happen to him after he died had always terrified him. Now that he knew exactly where he was going, the fear that pulsed through him was rich, tangible and made him restless.

Down the hall, he heard the mechanical sound of a door slowly opening and guessed that his long-awaited visitor had finally arrived. He peered through the window of his cell and saw Lawrence walking towards him. He stopped for a minute to talk to the guard, who opened up the door to David's cell. Rather than talking to David through the small door, Lawrence walked directly into the cell.

"Thanks, Bill," Lawrence said to the guard, "I can take it from here."

The guard nodded and walked the other way down the hall.

Lawrence, stuck his head out of the cell and waited until the guard was well out of site before turning back to David with a look of elation. "Well," he said with arms out as if expecting a hug from Estern. "We did it!"

"Yep, we certainly did," David responded not accepting the offer of the embrace.

"You're going on to great things! You are one of the chosen ones, the ones lucky enough to serve the Dark Lord. Your new life begins as soon as that poison goes through you tonight."

David winced and covered his head, sitting and running his hand over his hair.

He looked up and stared into the eyes of Lawrence Thompson. "I know what I did was wrong, I've come to terms with that, and I'm willing to accept my fate. I could have fought it. I could have shut the voices off. The reason why The Dragon spoke to us is because he knew we were weak. I don't know what they're gonna make me do while I am down there, but I know that will be my punishment for succumbing to evil."

"I think you're looking at this the wrong way." Thompson said.

"Well, let me tell you something that will possibly make you look at it the right way. No matter what happens to me down there, I'm going to do everything in my power to make sure you one day repent as well. I'm going to haunt you."

"You what?"

"As soon as I'm dead, I'm going to haunt you. I'm going to find a way to be that voice inside your head. The one that controls you and makes you do things you don't want to do. I'm going to be your punishment and haunt you 'til the day you die. Then, when you finally do, I'll be waiting there for you on the other side to do it all over again."

Thompson swallowed hard. "He'll never let you. He told me he'd protect me from anything if I helped you die."

"Repent, Lawrence," Thompson said. "God is the only one that can save you and you'd better start praying. If not, your new life of agony begins as soon as the poison hits my blood. Repent, or I will make sure Hell follows you wherever you go."

Shocked and terrified, Lawrence turned and stumbled out of the room as fast as he could, leaving David Estern alone again in his cell with nothing but regret, misery and a plan to someday make Lawrence Thompson feel the same.

They say the walk from the cell door to the execution chamber is one of the longest walks any person will ever take, not by distance, but by the length your mind perceives it to be. The Green Mile, The Long Haul, The Gallows March - call it what you will, it is a plodding and torturous journey. David Estern was trying to make his walk last as long as he could.

He tried to breathe in the air of the world one last time. But the musty atmosphere of the jail sucked through his nostrils and seemed to linger in his throat.

David thought about his life before the voices started. His job at the video production company had been sending him to various warehouses throughout New Jersey, where he would film and take pictures of equipment and machinery, later producing videos on how they worked. He had wanted to be a music video director once.

He slept alone, save for Paddy, his cat that he had adopted from a shelter a year earlier. He ate meals from the microwave, watched too much TV and internet porn and felt that each year he lived more of his former self died. Thinking back on his 30 years on the planet, he had the realization that he just might be better off.

Chapter 36

Dylan had been led through a series of dark, unmarked caverns by a pair of guards until he was stopped outside of a small wooden door, with a hazy window at the top marked "Office." He decided not to ask the guards where they were taking him, realizing that it most likely would not make sense.

He was still reeling from what he considered a near death experience. Had the weird man in the cape been trying to kill him? At the time it felt like he was being ripped apart from the inside. Now he didn't know what to think. As he pondered this, one of the guards came back though the office door and told the other guard that the counselor was ready for the prisoner and that Dylan could be brought through. Dylan took another sharp nudge to the back and walked through the open door.

Inside was a heavy-set man with thick glasses and a sloppily trimmed mustache sitting behind a desk rifling through a stack of papers. The door clicked behind him, and Dylan stood just outside of the doorway as he waited for the man to acknowledge him. After scribbling something on a piece of paper, counselor Stevenson looked up and motioned for Dylan to take a seat. Dylan walked to the desk and sat in one of the two chairs in front of the desk.

"So," the counselor began, "what can I do for you?"

"I'm not sure," Dylan said. "I'm pretty sure you wanted to see me."

"Oh, you're right. I'm sorry. I had you mixed up with someone else," the counselor said while rifling back through the stack of papers trying the find one that contained information on Dylan.

"You're one of them, right? A zoon, hence the big Z you had slapped on you."

"Excuse me? A what?"

"A zoon. Short for zoonosis, which is a parasite. It's the term we use when the living "infect" themselves into our environment. Not the most valorous term, I agree, but short, catchy and somewhat relevant."

"So I'm a parasite?"

"Try not to get wrapped up in the term, it really doesn't mean anything. What I'm more concerned with is what brought you down here in the first place. We try to talk to as many zoons, living people, as we can so we can try to prevent future infections. So what was it Mr. ..."

"James."

"Right, Mr. James. What was it that made you leave the beautiful, never-ending abyss of life to crawl down into the prison of the underworld? Please tell me you didn't do this on purpose, like some of them."

Dylan thought for a moment. "At first that was the plan," he said. "There was a girl who we thought needed help but then..." Dylan trailed off thinking about the events that led up to his descent into Hell. "My mom died," he said. "My mom died and then I was here. She killed herself."

Counselor Stevenson sighed and took a deep breathe. "I'm sorry to hear that, son. This place has a way of accepting the hopeless. It draws them in. I see it all of the time. Men with broken hearts, shattered dreams, misplaced plans. They all end up here. Now, let me inform you that if your plan was to come down here and find her, it's not very likely. The guards will ensure that you're kept under pretty constant supervision."

"Yeah, it was a stupid plan," Dylan said, thinking they were talking about Lauren. "I mean, I don't even know her that well. I just thought she was hot and I've been pretty lonely. Sad huh?"

"Your mother?" The counselor asked.

"What? No, the girl. I thought that's who you meant." The counselor sat back in his chair and waited for Dylan to realize what he was trying to tell him. "Holy shit!" Dylan said shooting up from his chair, "My mom is down here?!"

Chapter 37

Lauren was lying face down on her mattress in her cell and couldn't remember the last time she had felt so exhausted. The past week had been a series of tortures that left her body battered and her mind completely drained.

When she was alive, Lauren had a fear of heights so intense that she refused to ever live in any apartment that wasn't street level or below. Naturally, when she came to Hell, her torture centered on this fear. For years, Lauren was led to the top of a cliff and forced to look down at the 500-foot drop below. The exercise left her rattled and jittery and never got any easier. But recently, like Lauren had heard with every Inhabitant, her torture had gotten worse. At the beginning of the week, she was forced out to her ledge and stood there for a few tense moments overlooking the massive drop, but then she fell.

She had faced the ledge hundreds of times before with no incident, but this time she found herself plummeting down into the deep crevice. A living person would have been killed on impact, but when Lauren, being already dead, hit the ground, a wave of excruciating pain hit her body and pulsed through every inch of her as she lay in a dusty heap.

After gathering the strength to stand, she looked up towards the cliff she had fallen from and, while the summit was too far up to see, she could hear the faint laughter of the guard who had led her to the edge and, undoubtedly pushed her. Since then she had been led to the edge and pushed six other times. The pain never subsided, and her fear of heights only increased.

She lay motionless in her bed with arms hanging over the bed and her head buried deep in her pillow. She didn't think she could move if the room was on fire. She heard foot steps approaching her room, stopping at the door. A guard cleared his throat and shouted, "prisoner 666-534-5567. Please rise!" Lauren, as usual, decided to be insubordinate and stay perfectly still.

"What?" she said into her pillow.

"Please rise Ms. Adams," the guard said, not nearly as forceful this time. "Please?" he finally begged with a whimper.

Lauren braced herself slowly up with her hands, turned and sat on the edge of her bed. She had seen this guard before, as he usually patrolled her wing. She called him Lenny because he reminded her of the *Of Mice and Men* character, big, dumb and capable of choking a small animal to death. Next to him was a frail, terrified looking older woman in a sparkling new orange jump suit. She was trembling and wide eyed. The new Inhabitants always were.

"Who is this?" Lauren asked.

"Ms. Adams, this is your new roommate. Her name is...it's something with a G but that doesn't matter. She's gonna live with you now."

"A roommate? Since when do I need a roommate? I've been down here for almost seven years and I've never had to share a room with anyone. Is this part of the "new order?" Now I have to share my room with a senior citizen?"

"Not my problem," he said, throwing the terrified woman into the room and walking away.

Lauren studied the woman for a moment before rising off of her bed and approaching her. "Hi, I'm Lauren," she said extending a friendly hand. Despite no intention of hurting her, the woman jumped back out of the room, looked frantically down the passageway, got spooked by something else and then shot back inside Lauren's room.

"It's OK. It's OK," Lauren said. "I'm not gonna hurt you. I'm not one of them. I'm one of you." Lauren slowly put her hand out again and lightly touched the woman's arm. The woman, while still tense, seemed to relax a little, realizing that Lauren did indeed seem different from the gargantuan men with large weapons who had been shoving her around since she arrived here. "You killed yourself. That's why you're here, right?" Lauren asked. The woman nodded yes. "We all did, well, at least those of us on this side of Hell. What's your name?"

"Gace Games" the woman responded.

"Gace?" Lauren asked. "Your name is Gace? Are you European?"

"No!" the woman said visibly frustrated. She paused and sighed before pulling at her cheeks and over enunciating, "Grrrrrrrace. Grace," she concluded looking pleased with herself.

"Grace. Your name is Grace? That's pretty."

"Gank u," the woman responded. "Ah gad eh bet du, deh eh derr."

"Yeah. I bet you are," Lauren responded, even though she had no clue what the woman said.

"Well Grace, try to get some sleep while you can. They'll be around to torture the shit out of you at any minute."

"Tohter?" Grace said. Lauren did not respond and rolled over the wall, not wanting to speak to this strange woman anymore.

"Well this is fucking great," she whispered to herself. Lauren was understandably annoyed and confused by the woman's presence. Grace James had always had that effect on people, especially her son, Dylan.

Chapter 38

John and Chris were experiencing the reawakening. The sense of feeling began returning to their extremities as tiny pulses of electricity shot through them. Synapses returned to their brains, like lightening, recovering memories, characteristics and physical attributes. Their lives were flashing before them, in pieces, one at a time.

They had died in that pond, both of them. Their bodies still lay floating there, listlessly drifting, being smacked into from time to time by an occasional boat. Their spirits, however, had left the exhausted vessels and had attempted an escape into the next realm. Neither John nor Chris had led perfect lives, each guilty of all of the seven sins at some point. But, since they had never committed a mortal sin, their souls had planned to reinvent themselves in a new body and give each of them another chance at life. However, like every person in the underworld knows, there is no escape once you're inside. So, as hard as the two souls tried to reassemble their form in a new vessel, their efforts were in vain, and, since there was no way for them to rebuild, the spirits had no choice but to return to their original form and check into the underworld once and for all.

Chris's body was forming again, and, as his senses returned, he heard screaming and smelled something burning. His sight began to slowly return. What first presented itself as total blackness turned into blinding light, and his stomach twisted like he was careening down the first hill of a roller coaster. One final rush of energy and Chris was thrust through Hell's portal. Before he had a chance to realize what had just happened to him, he was kicked hard in the stomach, falling hard onto the rocky floor. Chris saw heavy black boots all around him, and most of them were coming at him from one angle or another hitting him on every inch of his body.

The owner of each set of boots was yelling something at him, but he could only decipher some if it and none of it was friendly: "Welcome to Hell, maggot!" "There is no escaping, stay down!" "Nice haircut, dip shit!" With each kick, his struggling subsided and he thought that they were actually breaking every bone in his body. He managed to gather enough strength to roll onto his other side and saw that John was laying on the ground ten feet away from him receiving similar treatment from another gang of boot-wearing Hell guards.

True to his character, John wasn't going down easy. "Fuuuuuck you! That's all you got, you pussies?" he was yelling as the guards grew increasingly frustrated, kicking him harder with each insult. "John!" Chris yelled. "Shut up!"

"Chris! Fuck you too!"

Chris then felt the kicking let up, and he was dragged to his feet. In front of him a guard menacingly glared at him while Chris was given a chance to catch his breath. He finally had time to realize that he was stark naked, as was John, who was still being kicked but had finally stopped hurling insults at his attackers.

"Put this on," the guard said to Chris, handing him a bright orange jumpsuit.

"I would love to," Chris said snatching the suit out of the guard's hands.

Chris saw John finally being forced to his feet and was given a suit of his own to put on. The two made weary eye contact with each other as John shrugged, not knowing just exactly how they had gotten there. He knew he lived a pretty shitty life but not one bad enough that he would be sentenced to Hell.

"Follow me," a guard said after the two were wearing the proper attire.

As two guards brought up the rear, John and Chris followed the lead guard as fast as their battered bodies could go. The show that was Hell's portal went on all around them, fire and brimstone and all.

"Chris," John whispered. "We got 'em right where we want 'em."

Chapter 39

Dylan had been led back to his cell and was angry. Knowing now that his mom was close by and in trouble, he was now more determined than ever. He was looking for Daman, the man that had only minutes before cast a spell on him and nearly killed him. He didn't know exactly what had happened, but he knew he could use him.

Dylan finally found Daman, the Devil, the former Dark Lord of the underworld, asleep at the back the cave with his head resting on Neville's lap.

"Hey!" Dylan shouted. "Wake the fuck up, man!"

"Shhhh," Neville said. "He's very exhausted. He needs his rest."

"I don't give a shit. Wake him up. He has some explaining to do. Hey, you! Wake up!" Dylan said delivering a jarring kick to Daman's backside.

"Oh, Jeemeany!" Daman cried out. "Oh eets you. Go away I sleep now," he said nuzzling back into Mr. Black's lap.

"No, you sleep later! What the hell was that? What were you doing to me back there? Who are you?"

Daman rolled over and looked sternly at Dylan. "I told you. I am heem, the Dark Lord. I am Satan, the ruler of dees place. At least I use to be."

"What do you mean by that? What do you mean used to be? Why are you in this cell if you are who you say you are?"

"There have been some changes," Neville said speaking on the Devil's behalf. "We believe we were sent down here because we had a difference of opinion with the man who thinks he is in charge of things. We are laying low until we figure out a plan."

"And this is your plan? You're napping? That's how you're going to be in charge again?"

"Da spell, it makes me very sleepy. I sleep now,' Daman said.

"The spell? You mean that shit you pulled on me? I felt like I was being ripped apart from the inside."

"I speak to your blood," Daman said. "It want to get out from you. I commanded it. You could have died."

"So what, you know magic?"

"Yes. Da dark magic. Very terrifying."

"Well, what are we waiting for? Use that shit on the guards? Let's get out of here! I have to find my mom, and you need to reclaim your throne. Let's go. Burn this mother down!"

Mr. Black lightly pushed Daman's head off his lap and rose to talk to Dylan. He walked over to him, put his arm around him and led him out of Daman's earshot. Daman appeared to have already fallen asleep again.

"Daman is a very powerful man. He ruled this section of Hell for centuries. While it's true he has powers that can bring this whole place crumbling down, his powers are very limited, and, well, he forgets a lot of them. They also make him very tired. He won't be able to do another spell for days."

"Days? Really? The most powerful man in the whole underworld? He can only make someone's blood dance around every couple of days? No wonder someone else took over."

"Please keep your voice down," Mr. Black said, leading Dylan even further away from the sleeping Devil. "The Dark Lord is very sensitive and he's had a really long day. We don't want to upset him."

Dylan thought about what had happened when Daman apparently tried to kill him. He remembered what was being said leading up to when Daman started to chant and apparently what had happened to make him unleash his magic. Dylan had a revelation. Upsetting the Dark Lord was exactly what he was going to do.

Dylan had nodded off for a bit but abruptly woke up when he heard the door to the cell banging open. The guards were coming to take someone away, and Dylan had a plan.

He made his way to the front of the cell and positioned himself so he was close to the guards but far enough away that he wouldn't be in their way. Two massive, no-neck guards stepped through the door and began looking around for whichever inmate they were summoned to retrieve. Dylan looked over at Daman and Mr. Black and saw that they, like all of the other people in the cell, were studying the guards intently, nervous about their mission. As the guards lazily walked further into the cell, Dylan decided to make his move.

"Excuse me," he said quietly enough that only the guards could hear. "Can I ask you guys a question?" The guards looked at Dylan and at each other with clear annoyance.

"Make it quick. We are here to retrieve a zoon for his official torture duty."

"Oh yeah. Of course, real quick. I'm just wondering what's up with the dude in the cape? You guys go to the circus and pick up the bearded lady?"

The two guards smirked a little bit before catching themselves and forcing their trademark scowls again.

"He's been down here for hours saying that he used to be in charge of everyone and that he used to order everyone around," Dylan continued. "If you ask me, the only guy he's in charge of is that little bitch in the suit that he's always cuddling with." Dylan made a subtle gesture over to Mr. Black but made sure he did so in a manner that neither could see him.

"Ha!" the guard on the left blurted out. "Yeah, those two were always so cute together. We always knew they were lovers."

Mr. Black and the Devil perked up, realizing the two guards were openly mocking them.

"We used to call them Thelma and Louise behind their backs," the other guard said. The two guards burst out in laughter and Dylan backed away into the shadows, hoping the inevitable would happen.

"What is theese, Leeeweese?" Daman said, rising and approaching the men.

"Oh just two ladies who end up going up in a fiery blaze of glory, just like you and your little lady are doing, only without the glory."

"Be careful," Daman said. "You do not want to upset ze dark magic."

"Ha! What are you going to do?" The guard on the left said. "Pull a rabbit out of Mr. Black's butt?" The two guards erupted in laughter, nearly falling over themselves, each having to hold the other one up.

"That'll do it," Dylan muttered as he quickly walked even further away from the guards, crouching down behind a bench, hoping to remain out of Daman's sight but still close enough to see what was going to happen.

Daman's eyes were glowing red and he was chanting, "Rakta, rudhira, loha, ha. Rakta, rudhira, loha, ha. Rakta, rudhira, loha, ha. Rakta, rudhira, loha, ha."

The guards stopped laughing, and panic washed over their faces. Daman continued to chant as the guard's eyes bulged and their veins pulsed and filled with blood. Around him, people began to take notice and started ducking down and taking cover like Dylan, as a low vibration shook the ground beneath them. One of the prisoners sidled up to Dylan, "What's he doing to them? What's gonna happen?" he asked.

"I'm not sure, but I think..." Before Dylan could finish, there was a loud pop, and the two guards literally exploded where they stood. Blood sprayed everywhere, coating the rocky walls with a sticky, crimson film. Pieces of skull and skin bounced around the cell like marbles.

Daman collapsed on the floor again, and for several moments everyone in the cell stayed completely silent and motionless. "Holy shit!" A voice at the back of the cell said. "That was bad ass!" The man who said it started slowly walking towards Daman and as he was doing so started clapping slowly urging those around him to do the same. Little by little the people in the cell started catching on, as the clapping turned from distinguishable single hits into an uproarious ovation, which shook Daman awake again. "Jeepers!" He said leaping to his feet. "What da heck happened?" "You did, sir!" Neville Black beamed proudly. "You're back!"

Dylan searched around the floor of the cell, rummaging through the carnage that used to be two full people. Under what looked like a part of an ear he found what he was looking for and proudly pulled up the keys that were once hooked to the guard's uniform. He walked over to the door, unlocked it and opened it proudly. "Anyone down for a little jail break?" he asked.

The plan that Dylan had hatched was not perfect, but he knew it would give them ample time to find the people they were looking for. Daman and Mr. Black needed to find the Dragon, and Dylan needed to find his mom. He had all but forgotten about Lauren, the woman that he had intended to rescue in the first place, and he had no idea that his mother and Lauren were together.

What they were going to do once they found who they were looking for was not completely hashed out. Dylan's plan involved escape and Daman's revenge.

With the help of Dylan, he had rediscovered some of his magic that made him Dark Lord of the underworld in the first place, but he insisted again that he was really too tired to do it this time. While he had also said this right before blowing up two people was something Dylan was aware of, he knew he needed a better plan than pointing at someone and asking for the Devil to make them explode.

Dylan was not completely surprised that out of the 50 or 60 people in the cell, only one of them, Acel, the French baker, actually wanted to escape. The rest of them did not want to return to their meaningless lives on Earth and claimed they were happier where they were. This was actually good news for Dylan, because it meant that they had little to lose and didn't mind being caught. With this in mind, Dylan gathered them all together and told them the plan.

"All of you will split up in groups of ten and stage mini prison-style riots all over this place. I mean get in there and just start wrecking shit! We need to get the guard's attention diverted towards you so the four if us can sneak around undetected and get to where we need to go."

"What if we get caught?" one of the men asked.

"Then you're probably gonna get beaten and tossed back in here. That's a small price to pay, knowing that you're finally making a difference for someone, right?"

"Ummm, I'm not so sure," said a voice from the back of the room. "I mean why should we help you?"

"Because, if you don't my friend here will blow you up. You don't want to make him angry do you?"

The men in the crowd looked at each and exchanged wordless glances. Daman looked on with a sinister stare. With the mob decidedly all on the same page, Dylan approached Daman, Mr. Black and Acel to fine-tune the rest of the details.

"So you're sure we can find out where my mom is, right?" he asked Mr. Black.

"We keep a record of every arrival in the office. At least we used to when we were in charge. We need to go find the counselor," he said.

"The guy in the office that does all of the intakes? I think I've been there. It's not far from here, right?" Dylan asked.

"Maybe a mile or so. If we send the crowd in the opposite direction, I think we can make it there without being detected," Neville said.

"And once we get there, then what? Won't the counselor just call the guards and turn us in?" Dylan asked.

"We don't believe that Jay has been turned yet. He was always a friend of ours, and we hope he still is," Neville responded.

"OK, let's just say he's not, though, and we get trapped in the office," Dylan said before turning to Daman. "Are you absolutely sure you're not ready to do the chanting, head exploding, blood thing yet?"

"Not yet, steel so tired," he said.

Dylan sighed, thinking how much easier this whole plan could be. "And him," Dylan said pointing to Acel. "He knows what we're doing? You told him `everything?"

"He make mistake by coming here," Daman said. "He want to live again." Damn looked at Acel and muttered something in French. Acel nodded his head. "Oui," he said.

"OK, let's do this then," Dylan said.

He walked back over to the crowd who looked antsy and excited. He looked over them and felt he should say something. "I'm not one for speeches," he began, "but I want to let you know that what you're about to do is important and...I just want to find my mom...I need to make some things right that I should have done a long time ago. I need to be a good son for the first time in a long time." Dylan sensed he was losing the crowd with his sappy speech. "So, let's go break some shit! Let's go!"

The crowd let out a roar as the first ten of the mob ran off down the corridor like escaping mental patients. Dylan waited ten seconds before sending off the second wave, then the third, then the fourth, and so on until the room was empty except for Daman, Neville Black, Acel and Dylan.

"Our turn," he said to them.

Chaos and destruction could be heard rattling throughout the underworld. The foursome ducked into a dark tunnel as a group of four guards ran towards the noise. The four men stepped out into the hallway and crept undetected towards their destination. Like parasites through a blood stream, ready to infect.

Chapter 40

Murderers, rapists, terrorists and psychopaths were arriving in droves through the portal. Most of them were there because of some villainous act that the Dragon had possessed them to do. He was waiting at the portal and personally greeting each of them as they entered. His crowning achievement, David Estern, who was walking down a hallway to meet his death, had not yet arrived.

Gregory Irons was seeing his plan reach fruition. He had overthrown the Devil and was currently in the midst of sculpting Hell into his personal vision: a place devoid of apathy and mercy. A physical embodiment of the consequences of committing a sin on earth and he was the leader of it all. It was the stuff of legends. People would remember his name. Once he fashioned the Hell under New Jersey to behave this way, then he would take his army and move throughout the underworld, taking control over every part of it. He would become a god. The thought of it made the hairs on his neck stand up with excitement.

He had been at the portal all day awaiting David Estern's arrival. In that time, he had greeted 30 other Puppets, as he had taken to calling them. They were angry and possessed soldiers who would do his every bidding. A few other assorted guards were milling around the area, and they too were under the Dragon's evil command.

There was a popping sound and the portal erupted into a blinding flash of light. Someone was coming.

"Alright, chaps! Look alive!" Irons said to the guards. "I think we got one."

The portal made a sucking sound, and a naked man shot though the portal onto the floor. Irons recognized him immediately. It was Peter Timpton, a former mechanic he had commanded to cut the brakes on a series of cars he had at his shop. All the cars were involved in accidents just blocks away from the shop, and several people died. By the time the cops traced the accidents to his shop, Peter had died by closing the garage doors to his shop, running the remaining cars and inhaling the exhaust. Peter, like everyone who was shot through the portal, bounced up quickly, wild eyed and in attack position.

"Right on time. Welcome, ol' boy!" the Dragon shouted at him. Peter stopped his protesting, clearly recognizing the Dragon's voice from inside of his head. It was the voice that brought him here and now the voice that was greeting him on the other side.

"It's you," Peter said. "I'm not crazy. You're really here!"

"Of course I am, ol' boy. I told you I'd be here. Sorry for the mess up there. It's just we needed you down here, and we have to go about it in creative ways."

"So what do you need me to do? What is my purpose?"

"Well, first we're going to get you some proper attire," the dragon said, motioning to Peter's naked body. "Then we'll tell you all about it. It will be big. Geezers will remember you forever! Guards, please lead Mr. Timpton to his new home, and make sure his uniform is extra bright and crisp."

"Thank you," Peter said to the Dragon, clearly believing that he was exactly where he needed to be. Irons gave him a wordless nod as he was led away. He smiled to himself, pleased with the work he had done.

David Estern was to be the last arriving soldier and, according to the sheriff's calculations, would be arriving in at least another hour.

Even underworld dictators need rest and the sheriff rationalized that he deserved an hour to lie down before his protégé arrived and the real work began.

Chapter 41

John and Chris were seated in front of the counselor who was beyond puzzled.

"So you say you died down here, drowned in Styx Pond and that sent you through the portal?"

"Those were our evil twins," John said, trying the old standby one more time.

"John, not now," Chris said. "That's what happened. My friend here just couldn't keep his mouth shut, and those fishermen attacked us. We both fell out of the boat and drowned, I guess. That's the last thing we remember."

"I'm just confused because we know, at all times, the activity of the portal. No one comes through the portal without our knowledge, yet, here you are."

"So what does that mean for us?" Chris asked.

"I'm not rightly sure," the counselor said. "Normally, we would throw you in with the others, but your circumstance is interesting. And, with the way the Dragon's been these days, I doubt even he cares at this point. I'm not even sure what my future is anymore. I've been down here all day and you're the first clients that have come into my office. It's like he's phasing me out."

From outside the office, shouting could be heard, followed by the sound of things being broken and destroyed.

"What in the world?" the counselor said opening the door to his office and looking up and down the hallway. The two guards who were usually positioned outside his office were gone, and Jay thought he saw their shadows running in the opposite direction chasing after something. Not wanting to concern himself any further, he backed into his office and closed the door behind him. He turned back towards Chris and John and shrugged.

From behind him, the door he had just shut creaked slowly open. Mr. Black peaked his head though the door and tried to get the counselor's attention.

"Pssst. Jay, it's me."

Jay turned to see Neville's tiny egg head.

"What are you doing here? How did you get out?" Jay said.

"We escaped. I have others with me. Can we come in?"

"Yes! Get in here quickly and close the door."

Neville turned and whispered something to the others who were still out of sight. He then walked through the door, followed by Daman, Acel and Dylan. It was a joyous reunion for all.

"Daman!" Jay said.

"Dylan!" Chris said.

"Chris!" Dylan said.

"Dylan!" John said.

"John!" Dylan said.

"Jay!" Daman said.

"Acel!" Acel said, raising his hand in an attempt to join the celebration. No one seemed to care that he was there, and he felt left out.

Everyone in the room embraced as the different groups of friends were elated that they were reunited.

"We need your help, Jay," Mr. Black finally said.

Everyone involved took turns explaining to the others how they had arrived there, except of course for Jay who had been there all day with no break. Neville and Dylan took turns explaining to Jay how they needed to know the whereabouts of Dylan's mom and Gregory Irons.

"I can help you find the woman, but I wouldn't recommend going after Irons. He's amassing an army that gets stronger by the day, and all of that power has gone to his head. I just don't think you are powerful enough to defeat him. You're just not strong enough, Daman."

A flash of red shot over Daman's eyes. "Not yet," he said sternly, "but I will be very soon."

"I'd trust him if I were you. I've seen what he can do when he's pissed," Dylan said.

"Your mom is with Ms. Adams, who's a friend of mine. She's safe. She's with the suicides. I think with the chaos you've created outside you should be able to get to her with no problem. Getting her out of here could be problem, though, and I'm not sure it's even possible. As I told you before, once you're here, you're here for good."

"We'll cross that bridge when we come to it. I have a feeling there's some magic hidden deep inside of this guy that can help us figure out all of this at some point," Dylan said patting Daman in the stomach.

"I know how I can take away the attention of the remaining guards," Jay said. He pressed down the intercom button at his desk and said "All guards in Sector 5, please report to my office for emergency staff training. Repeat. All Sector 5 guards to my office."

"That's it?" Dylan said.

"That's it," Jay said. "What are you waiting for? Go! Stay in the shadows. They'll be coming this way. Daman and Mr. Black will show you the way. Please be careful. Go!"

Joined now by Chris and John, the group of men thanked Jay Stevenson and slipped out the door.

They huddled in the closest unused corridor they could all fit in and waited for herds of guards to pass by on their way to the counselor's office for their contrived staff meeting.

When the coast was clear, they emerged from their hiding place and rushed towards the suicide section of the underworld. Dylan quickened his pace and urged the others to do the same. He was going to save his mother successfully this time.

Fifteen of the Sector 5 guards crammed into the counselor's office, waiting to hear what he had to say. Their job had changed considerably since the Dragon took over, so they thought they were here to learn more about new policies and tactics. They had no idea that they were being held there by Jay in order to make sure his friends could roam the halls of Hell free and clear.

"Welcome, welcome" Jay began. He paused for an uncomfortably long time, making eye contact with all of the guards and killing as much time as he could. "I'd like us not to think of this as a training session but more as a general meet and greet, just a quick rap session to see how everyone is doing."

Jay sat on his desk like the cool high school guidance counselors he had always wanted to be when he was alive, slipping a bit as he tried to put his hand down and adjust himself. "So let's rap. How is everyone?"

The guards looked around befuddled, none of them knowing how to respond.

"You," Jay said pointing to the biggest and dumbest looking guard in the room. "What about you, everything going OK?"

"Me?" he said pointing to his chest.

"Yeah, you. What's your name?"

"Gabrielle," he said. "No one ever really asked me that in a while."

"And how does that make you feel?"

Gabrielle thought long and hard before answering, "Bad?"

"Yeah, I could imagine that. You feel like no one cares about you, that you're just a hired gun?"

"It's like nothing we do is good enough," one of the guards from the back said. "I tortured an Inhabitant for six hours today. I had blisters all over my hands from whipping him, and the Dragon didn't even say I did a good job. The Devil used to reward us." The rest of the guards nodded in agreement.

He hadn't intended this originally, but Jay could sense that these hardened guards, like him, were not happy with the new regime. Perhaps he could talk these men into helping Daman and the others. He needed to dig deeper.

"Ah yes, Daman, the Devil. He is a good man, a fair man. And now, where is he? Locked in a cell somewhere, rotting, along with Neville Black. Powerless and alone, just like all of you."

Jay sensed a feeling of shame from the guards. Several of them put their heads down and let out heavy sighs. He was reeling them in, and now he just had to set the hook. He had never incited a riot before, but he could feel that he was on the right track.

"What else do we think was better when the Devil was in charge?" A number of hands shot up, and, as he was about to call upon one the guards, the door to his office swung open and the Dragon burst into the room.

"What the bloody hell is this? There are groups of prisoners literally ripping this place apart, and you lot are in here singing *Kumbaya*! Get out there and take control!"

The guards quickly jumped up from their chairs and ran out of the room, not wanting to upset the Dragon any further. While it appeared they were fed up with him, they still feared him. When they were all gone, he turned and glared at the counselor.

"You," he said, "just what do you think you're doing, Stevenson?"

"Just talking to the troops. Trying to raise morale. "

"While you're raising morale, prisoners are running all over the place like someone opened the primate paddock at the Daisy Store!"

"The what, sir?" Jay asked.

"The monkey cage at the zoo! Daisy store is what people call it where I'm from...England!"

"I've never heard that before."

"Does it bleeding matter, ya bleeding turkey?"

"No sir, it does not. Anything I can do to help, sir?"

"Yes, come with me. I need you to make sure everything runs smoothly when Estern arrives. It's about time you made yourself useful."

The Dragon grabbed Jay by the arm and rushed him out of the door. Jay wasn't sure where the Dragon was taking him, but he was happy he was getting out of the office for a change.

Chapter 42

Dylan and the others snuck their way past hordes of escaped prisoners and guards all the way to the suicide section. Along the way, they cringed at the site of prisoners being captured and savagely beaten by guards. Although they felt sympathy, they were grateful that, because of this, they had traveled the whole way totally undetected. Nothing takes away a person's focus more than beating someone senseless.

The counselor had told them the exact location of Dylan's mother, and the group rounded the bend to her quarters. Inside, Lauren and Grace lay on their bunks, exhausted from their days of torture.

"Spiders, huh?" Lauren said to Grace. "Yeah, that's a bitch, I can't believe they can know so much about us. So they just kept dropping them on you?"

"Dah, oder and oder," Grace said.

Over the course of the few hours they had spent together, Lauren had actually gotten quite used to Grace's distinctive way of speaking. She thought she could understand pretty much everything she was saying, and even when she couldn't she pretended she could. She had never had a companion her entire time in the underworld, and having someone to talk to, no matter how confusing it got at times, was refreshing. She felt compassion for the woman and liked looking after her.

"I wish I could tell you it gets easier, but it won't. It will just get worse. Something about being down here just won't allow your mind to talk you out of the terror. Let's just enjoy these relaxing moments while the fucking Dragon still allows them. I never thought I'd say this, but I miss the Devil."

"Da Devil is closer than you think," Daman said. "Now rise and bow before him once again!"

Startled, the two women bolted upright. "You?" She said at his approach. "They said you were dead." Neither Lauren nor Grace could yet see behind Daman, as he blocked the cell door with his cape obscuring their view.

"Dey said? Who is dey?" Daman asked.

"I don't know. Everyone! They say the Dragon killed you and that creepy guy you were always hanging out with!"

Daman's eyes flashed red with anger again.

"Oh, I'm not dead either," Neville said, poking his head around Daman. "It's all a big misunderstanding. We're here to reclaim the Devil's throne and to rescue her," Neville said pointing to Grace. Lauren turned to look at Grace, whose facial expression changed from utter confusion to elation and joy. This change in moods was because her son Dylan and his childhood friend John were emerging from behind Daman.

"Deeyan!" she cried, exploding off of her bunk and rushing into his arms.

"Mom!" Dylan said.

"Mrs. James!" John said.

"John!" Grace said.

"You guys?" Lauren said as she recognized her valiant gift shop employee.

"You?" Dylan said, finally remembering Lauren's existence but confused as to why she was with his mother.

"You came for me!" Lauren said as she too rushed to embrace Dylan.

"Um, yeah. That's it. We did it. Here we are. Um, how do you two know each other?"

Before she could answer, a visibly excited Grace interjected. "Ater I cude nt tal to u I deacekd to dah. Ten I end up in he. De na. He swe me heah. Rajel, hd bee taka cer oe ma."

"Mom, slow down, I can't understand you. What happened?" he asked, looking at Lauren for clarification.

"She say dat after she try to call you, she decide to end eet," Daman began. "She somehow end up here. Da man she speak to send her here weeth Lauren. She take care of her."

"You can understand her?" Dylan asked. "You got all of that?"

"I tell you before dat I speak all da lenguages, except de Spanish."

"I lah you, Dian," Grace said.

"She say she love you," Daman said.

"Yeah, I figured out that much," Dylan said.

"So, wait. How did you know she would be with me?" Lauren asked.

"I didn't, but I'm glad you are," said Dylan not knowing know what to say. He usually froze up around girls he liked, and, as he looked on at Lauren in all her beautiful deadness, he realized he had never heard her speak and had a million things he wanted to ask her. "How's your neck?" he asked her, rubbing the back of his own remembering the deep cuts she had carved into it.

"Oh, it's fine," she said. "I heal pretty quickly. How's your head?"

"I've had worse," he said.

They smiled at each other, but the moment was quickly broken up by the sound of another poor prisoner being beaten savagely.

"They're getting closer," Chris said. "We gotta go."

"But where?" Dylan said. "What's the plan?"

"It's not safe here," Neville said. "We have to move. Dylan, we helped you get this far, now help us finish it. We need to find the Dragon."

"He's been at the portal all day," Lauren said. "He's waiting for some guy named Estern. Everyone has been talking about it."

"Perfect, that's exactly where we want him."

Chapter 43

David Estern stared at the ceiling from his spot on the gurney and waited for the sodium thiopental to offer it's sweet release. He was hooked up to a series of IVs connected to tubes that shot out of him like wires. He was a disassembled robot, more machine than human. He inhaled deeply and caught the familiar scent of rubbing alcohol. At least it would be clean.

In the underworld, the welcome group was just outside of the portal area and were watching from afar as Gregory "the Dragon" Irons, aka Steven Arby, addressed the room full of guards. Counselor Stevenson stood nervously by his side.

"Today marks a new chapter in the history of the underworld. Soon to come through that portal is a man that has shown himself to be callously evil, unscrupulously cold and most importantly, obedient. As we march through the caverns of Hell, it is people like David Estern and the rest of the new Inhabitants that will ensure a new dominion and solidify my place, I mean our place, as the man who changed the underworld. The old and ineffective ways of the Devil are gone and forgotten. Let the fires rage through the caverns and spill onto the moist, pink belly of the Earth! This is our time to conquer and destroy!"

The gathered guards let out an apathetic cheer.

"Is that the best you can bleeding do? I said destroy! The Devil's reign is over!" At the tail end of the last syllable, the Dragon's voice cracked ever so slightly.

The guards cheered apathetically again.

Dylan looked at Daman, whose eyes were glowing a furious red. He knew what he needed to do next. His group had made their way to the portal area and were hiding behind a series of rocks still within ear shot of the Dragon.

"You hear that?" he whispered to him. "That fucking limey imprisoned you, took away your power and is now talking shit about you. Are you gonna let him do that?"

"No," Daman said, his veins filling wide with blood. The air grew colder and the lights flickered. The Devil was about to show his power.

Chapter 44

The injection would come in three stages. David's body would first accept a dose of sodium thiopental, which would render him unconscious. This would be followed by some pancuronium bromide, which would paralyze his muscles, and finally a shot of potassium chloride would stop his heart.

To the left of him, David could hear warden Dormeus's voice but could not make out any of the words he was saying. They were fuzzy and hovered in the air. Was he dying? Was he already dead? From the other side of him another person approached the gurney and stopped at his midsection. He turned his head to see a man in a white coat holding a syringe. It was time.

The man securely grabbed his wrist, and David felt the familiar pinch of a needle. He knew it was only a matter of seconds now and, despite his assertion that he was beyond being saved, David Estern decided now was the time to ask for forgiveness.

"Forgive me, Father, for I have sinned," he began. "Please help me as I..." he began to get drowsy and could not remember the The Lord's Prayer. "I'm sorry," he said just before drifting off to sleep.

The subsequent injections occurred and after several minutes the heart monitor lay flat and unblinking.

David Estern was dead.

Chapter 45

"No, no, no, no!" The Devil chanted as he rose from his hiding place, walking slowly towards the Dragon with a new found determination and drive that he had lost long ago. The throngs of guards who were sworn to protect the Dragon parted like leaves, allowing their former master safe passage. They looked on with respect and admiration.

"No, no, no, no," the Devil continued as he approached his nemesis, the Dragon, who looked on with a mixture of confusion, humor and just a touch of panic.

"What's this then?" He chuckled, "the little school girl returns, trying to teach daddy a lesson? What've you got this time, dearie?"

"Rakta, rudhira, loha, ha. Rakta, rudhira, loha, ha. Rakta, rudhira, loha, ha," Daman chanted.

"Fuck yes," Dylan said to the remaining group still hiding behind him. "Watch this."

The Dragon's mocking laughter suddenly stopped as a jolt passed through him. His blood had begun it's unstoppable quest of leaving his body.

"What're you doing? What is this?" He asked as his veins swelled with blood. He opened his mouth to speak again but his voice was cut off by the rising fluid. A tiny tear of crimson trickled from his mouth.

Dylan had initially feared that the Dragon would be too powerful for the Devil, but, as he watched him twitch and convulse, he knew this was clearly not the case.

He looked at the throng of guards. Some watched with delight, some watched with fear, some watched with a mixture of both, but none came forward to help their new leader.

Dylan saw many familiar faces. He saw the guard from the elevator, the two guards that had marched him down the hall into the cell, several he now recognized from his days of watching the line on Earth and the two guards the Devil had exploded in the cell. That was them, right? But how were they here? They had died. He had watched it. He looked over at Chris and John. They had told him about how they died and were thrust back through the portal. He gathered that the same thing had happened to them. There's no escaping Hell when you die. You just come right back.

He looked back at the Dragon, whose eyes were filling with a deep, burning red. They were ready to burst out of their sockets, prompting the rest of the blood to follow. The Dragon would soon be completely eviscerated.

"Oh no," Dylan said to no one. "This isn't going to work."
The Dragon's body, not being able to withstand the strain anymore, exploded. The nearby guards, as well as Jay Stevenson, all shielded their eyes with their hands, hoping to avoid the onslaught of bone, blood and brain matter.

Daman hit the ground in a heap. His cheek pressed hard on the slick surface as he let out slow, deliberate breaths. A shocked murmur pounced through the on lookers. They did not know if they should be jubilant or angry.
What happened next was no surprise to Dylan.

The portal began to surge and pop with the anticipation of a new Inhabitant. With a familiar flash of light, the portal opened fully, dropping Gregory Irons's newly formed, freshly killed body back into Hell.

The guards returned to formation and Dylan and his friends jumped back behind the rock they were hiding behind. The Dragon jumped fast to his feet and looked angrily over the crowd.

"Are you freakin' kidding me? What kinda bullshit are we talking about here?"

The Dragon's body looked the same to the puzzled crowd, but somehow his voice had changed and his accent was gone. The shock of dying for a second time and the blind rage that followed it shocked Gregory "the Dragon" Irons out of his system. Steven Arby was all that remained, and his native New Jersey accent shone through as he berated the room like an incensed Woody Allen.

"This is the freakin' thanks I get? You freakin' ungrateful assholes! This was my moment, and you all ruined it! Arrest him!" he said, pointing to Daman who was still passed out. "Arrest all of them. What am I, a schmuck? You think I can't see you hiding behind that rock? Arrest them? Rain fire from the sky!" When voiced in his Dragon persona, lines like this carried some frightening weight, but, in his natural voice, everything he was saying was light, airy and comical. It didn't help his cause that he was naked either. The building of laughter danced around the crowd.

"Don't you dare laugh at me! No one laughs at Steven Arby and gets away with it...I mean Gregory Irons, the freakin' Dragon. Fuck you!"

The laughter grew louder as the guards resorted to giving each other high fives and pointing at Steven's genitals.

"Stop it! Stop laughing!" he protested.

From behind him, the portal started opening up again. The loud popping cut through the laughter, diverting the guards' attention away from Steven Arby's naked body and towards its beckoning call. David Estern had finally arrived.

"You hear that? That's who I really need! This guy is gonna make all of you pussies wish you were never born! He is my Puppet and will do anything I want. I don't need any of yous! None of yous!"

He raised his arms and turned away from the audience and towards the portal. It furiously sparked and popped ready to deliver David Estern to his predestined new home.

Dylan started to panic. He didn't know what was coming through the portal. He only hoped that whatever it was was not powerful enough to help this raving lunatic regain his power. He held his breath in anticipation. His heart pounded rapidly.

The initial strands of blinding light raced through the portal as David Estern's body was beginning to materialize.

Steven Arby, wild eyed and more bent on revenge than ever, stepped closer to the portal. He was so blinded with anger that he did not notice Jay Stevenson, mild-mannered underworld counselor, take a few seemingly innocent steps towards him. As the final pulsing sound filled the room, Jay Stevenson stepped right behind the dictator formerly known as the the Dragon and pushed him.

Steven Arby, unaware of Jay's presence, completely lost his balance and fell forwards into the portal. He collided with David Estern and the two tumbled into the deep nothingness of the portal until they were out of view.

Bands of light pulsed through the portal and a jet-engine roaring sound filled every crevice of the underworld before stopping and leaving the room in snow-fallen silence. One final tiny mouse fart of a sound was emitted before the portal closed in on itself.

The room waited for something to happen. They waited for the portal to open back up and for the Dragon to appear again, only this time fused with whatever was on its way through the portal, bigger, stronger, and angrier. They waited. But nothing came.

Out of the pack of guards, Boggins, the biggest and meanest of the guards, shoved his way to the front of the crowd. He scowled as he passed Dylan and the others and stopped just shy of counselor Stevenson, whose hand was still frozen in the position when he had pushed Steven Arby into the portal. "What did you do?" Boggins asked him.

"Well, I uh...sent him away, I suppose," Jay answered.

"He's not coming back?" Boggins asked.

"Well, not any time soon."

Boggins's cold scowl turned upwards into a slight smile. He extended his hand out to Jay Stevenson, who nervously grabbed it and shook it. Boggins turned back towards the rest of the guards. "Do you hear that?" he yelled. "The Dragon is fucking gone!" The guards erupted in celebratory applause. Hugging each other and jumping up and down. A group of them rushed Jay Stevenson, grabbing him and hoisting him on their shoulders. He was a hero. The other guards, realizing that Jay did not do this alone, started a familiar chant.

"Hail Satan! Hail Satan! Hail Satan!"

The Dark Lord had regained power, but was at the moment still resting from his dark magic. The commotion woke him up. "Ohh deery!" Neville ran over and crouched beside him. "Did we keel him? He is gone?" Daman asked.

"You got him, sir, He's gone."

"So I will rule again?"

"Well if the crowd is any indication, I think that's a possibility. Listen to them!"

Daman listened to the guards chant and looked on with admiration. He felt like a new Devil. He stood up triumphantly and, while spreading his cape wide and proud, walked into the crowd of worshipers. "My frehnds! I have returned! Come now! Shoot your love all over me."

Almost a perfect moment.

Finally being let down by the guards, Jay approached Dylan and friends, beaming and walking taller than he ever had before. "Did you see me? I did it! Hey, you found your mom," he said to Dylan. "I can't believe you did that," Lauren said, rushing Jay and hugging him tightly. "Did you have that planned the whole time?" "No. I mean I thought it might work. What other choice did we have at that point?"

"So, where did he go?" John asked. "Is he dead?"

"I'm not entirely sure," Jay said. "There are other realms far beyond this one that the portal leads to. He is most likely on his way to one of them. How long he stays there is anybody's guess. For now, we're safe."

"So is that how we get out?" Dylan asked. "We can all jump through the portal and get back to earth?"

"Get out?" Jay asked. "Why whatever do you mean?"

"I mean, like escape. Will the portal work for me and my mom and my friends?"

Jay put his arm around Dylan and walked him away from the group. "Your friends are dead Dylan. They can't leave here. Even if we allowed you all to walk out the front door, you would eventually come back. The spirit that built this place will always call you back. It doesn't let go of anyone."

"Well, what about the portal? It worked for that English dude."

"It's not safe Dylan. There is no telling where you will end up and in what form. If you go through that portal, life as you know it will cease to exist. It will transform it into something new."

"So we're stuck here? Well that's just fucking great. We need to get back home!"

Jay took his arm off of Dylan and looked at him, "Why?" he asked. "What is there to return to?"

"Well," Dylan began, "my uhhh...there's the...thing...." He stopped and pondered this for a few more moments before realizing he couldn't settle on one single solitary thing that was worth returning to. "Touché, sir," he said to Jay.

Dylan turned back around and looked at the rest of the group. He smiled as his mother, his two best friends and the girl he had been in love with for a while were all talking to each other. It was the most friends he had had together in a long time.

Dylan felt an initial surge of panic blow over him before something quickly chased it away. He thought about his dead-end life on Earth and the aisles of disappointments. He thought about the daily pressures he was faced with and the terror of never living up to expectations.

"Fuck it," he said. "I guess I'm staying here then."

He looked up at the buzzing track lighting of the room that ran in an infinite line across the underworld and inhaled a deep whiff of sulfur. He was finally home.

Chapter 46

The labor had been long and strenuous on Molly Ortega, but she was in its final stages and her husband, Paul could see their child's head crowning.

"You can do it honey!" he shouted. "We're almost there! Keep pushing."

Molly responded with a series of shouts, screams and with one final push, their first born son was born.

Paul, a fiercely religious man, looked up to the Heaven's and mouthed an inaudible "thank you," before kneeling down before his wife's bed.

The child, who they had already named Daniel, was beautiful! Olive complexion and minty green eyes were offset by scattered wisps of black hair. He was as healthy as they come and almost perfect.

But what grew inside the boy, inside the deepest caverns of his heart, was pure evil. Steven Arby's corrupt and tainted soul travelled from the underworld, through purgatory and back onto Earth. It hovered for a bit before settling on a new place to rest inside the body of Daniel Ortega.

His parents cried tears of joy at the birth of their first son, having no way of knowing that the soul now trapped inside their infant son was dark, calculated and full of hate. The damned soul lay dormant inside the new, tiny vessel, waiting patiently for the next chance to unleash it's fury on the world.

No one would ever laugh at Daniel Ortega.

Chapter 47

Lawrence Thompson awoke to a sound. The voice of the Dragon had inexplicably stopped after the execution and he had all but forgotten about it, returning to his normal sleep patterns. But here, in the peaceful night, something beckoned from the deep caverns of his mind and called to him by name.

"Lawrence," it said.

He shot up quickly and looked around the room. Knowing this time where the voice was coming from, he knew that further investigation was unnecessary. "Hello?" he said. "Who's there? Is it you? I can hear you. Do you need me again master?"

There was a pause and then the voice began laughing a calculated, prickly laugh.

"Who is this?" Lawrence Thompson asked.

"It's me," David Estern said. "I told you I'd do it. I found you."

Chapter 48

Dylan and Lauren had decided to take a walk. Hand in hand, they had walked through the underworld, Lauren pointing out various landmarks along the way.

They passed by the cliff she had been forced to fall from time and time again. She laughed as she told him about the nightmares that cliff had caused. She gripped his arm and felt safe. It didn't seem too threatening anymore.

Dylan had told her he was afraid of heights too. They found out they had a lot more in common as they walked. They both liked music but hated musicians, liked sports but couldn't stand athletes, liked sex but hated dating. They were two peas in a pod, which they also hated.

They walked further through Hell's passages, eventually winding up at the shore of Styx Pond.

"Whoa, what's this?" Dylan asked looking out over the ever stretching body of water and marveling at the hundreds of boats that glided across its smooth surface.

"Just another ploy by the powers-that-be to make life down here intolerable. I think this was one of the Devil's ideas actually."

"It's actually sort of pretty," Dylan said.

"Is it? How about now?" Lauren said as she pointed to the washed up corpses of Chris and John.

"Oh shit!" Dylan said, jumping back. "Is that..." Dylan had never seen a dead body before, much less the bloated corpses of two of his friends. "What are those stains on their pants? Did they..." he asked.

"It's just a part of death, Dylan." Lauren said.

"Ah, they won't mind," Dylan said.

"Won't mind what?" Lauren asked.

"If we do this," Dylan said as he leaned in and kissed Lauren deeply. "Well, the way me met may have been a little unorthodox, but I think we're off to a good start."

"I'd say so," Lauren said, feeling genuine affection towards this dopey gift-shop guy. While her rescue from Hell wasn't exactly the stuff of fairy tales, it had worked out for her in the end. Maybe she could finally be happy.

"Let's get out of here," Dylan said taking Lauren's hand in his again.

They took a few steps before Dylan stopped and turned to face her. "I know it's really none of my business, but I've always been curious. What exactly did you do that made you end up down here?"

Lauren pulled her hand back from Dylan and looked at him stone faced. "I killed my ex-boyfriend," she said flatly before walking away.

Dylan did not follow her. Instead, he turned back to the shore of Styx Pond and looked over the water. The air was calm and the ripple of water tickled the bottom of the rowboats.

At this point, Dylan James realized that he had made a terrible, terrible mistake.

Made in the USA
San Bernardino, CA
25 September 2013